CHASING

A Novel by Ronald Wallingford

For Lucille.

The author wishes to thank Frank M. Tierney and W. Glenn Clever for their guidance of the manuscript through to its printing. Marj Kelly edited an early edition of the manuscript. Michelle Porter and Maureen Stapleton Hay provided valuable comments on the text.

CHASING

A Novel by Ronald Wallingford

BOREALIS

Borealis Press Ltd.
Ottawa, Canada
2003

Canada

The Publishers acknowledge the financial assistance of the Government of Canada through the Book Publishing Industry Development Program (BPIDP) for our publishing activities

National Library of Canada Cataloguing in Publication Data

Wallingford, Ronald, 1933–
Chasing / Ronald Wallingford.

ISBN 0-88887-185-6

I. Title.

PS8595.A57C46 2003 C813'.54 C2003-901273-5
PR9199.3.W34735C46 2003

Cover illustration by Roxanne Borris
Design and typesetting
by Chisholm Communications, Ottawa

Printed and bound in Canada on acid-free paper

Table of Contents

Chapter

Chapter 1

"Good God, that's the swimmer Alex Baumann," cross-country skier Arvo mutters as he gazes at the scarlet maple leaf embroidered on Baumann's golf shirt.

"Geez," gasps first year student Gavin recalling the telecast of Baumann's slash through water to set a world record in the individual medley, "Wasn't it cool him developing that ability at this university?"

"Ah, hell," Windsor freshman Scott, a shot putter, quips, "he was born with a knack for swimming and a touch of instruction brought it out."

"Bull!" Lanky Arvo growls from across the table, "Do you know how hard that guy trained?"

"What's that?" Scott says, inflating his prodigious chest.

Arvo chuckles in an attempt to defuse the situation but adds, "When I worked at the athletic equipment counter, Baumann changed towels two and three times a day."

Scott's pupils enlarge; he grips each arm of his chair and leans toward Arvo; perspiration crawls into the creases of his forehead. An explosion of rock music diverts the debate.

Onlooker Gavin, a tousled-haired freshman from North Bay, is fascinated by Arvo's inference on Baumann. He wonders, surely Alex Baumann conceals no secrets. If he can chase world records, someone else in his own sport must be able to do the same. Arvo, a nationally ranked cross-country skier, can't be talking nonsense.

Scott eases his eighty-five kilogram mass to the back of his chair and stretches his arms overhead. His fingers interlock as he pulls. Following a full extension, Scott says, "Of course Baumann does a bit of work, but he's so good it's easy; it wouldn't be like one of us trying to swim that much."

"Naturally," Arvo says, "he's good because the more he does the stronger he gets. And the more—" Arvo's voice drops when he notices Scott's eyes shift to a young lady in tight jeans pulling up a chair at the next table.

Gavin, reflecting on the previous discussion, pauses; his facial muscles move as though rehearsing his wording before he says, "You know somethin', I used to run—could manage a fast 1,500-metres."

Both corners of Scott's thick lips sag as he turns to Gavin and says, "Horse manure; I saw you dragging ass in that touch football game during the freshman bash; you couldn't break six minutes for 1,500-metres."

Gavin jumps to his feet, clenches his teeth, jabs his right hand into his front pocket and tosses a scrunched bill on the table. "This ten says I can break an even five—right now!"

"Easy, easy," Arvo says with a curious smile, and adds, "this fall's varsity track trials are tomorrow. They're open to anyone who shows up; try it then Gavin?"

Gavin shrugs. They both gaze at Scott.

Scott frowns like a baby overdue for a diaper change, pauses and reaches into his blue denim shorts. He slaps a bill on the table and says, "Okay *Northern Dancer,* this ten says you can't."

In residence, a half-hour before the race, Gavin searches his closet for spiked shoes. He yanks at stray laces and boots fly out. Successful his second attempt, he wonders what shorts he will wear. A glance at his cutoff jeans assures him they will have to do.

He sighs on arriving at the athletic building for he remembers shorts are issued with the athletic kits. Gavin changes, stuffs his clothes into his locker and jogs to the track.

When Gavin approaches, Arvo hollers, "I've already registered you."

Gavin nods, sits on a bleacher step and rams his toes into racing shoes. Two squawking ravens cavorting on the floodlights above him distract his calculation as to what pace he dare try the first two laps. In snug spikes he runs easily on grass for seven minutes before the starter commands, "Sweats off."

Gavin jerks his Widdifield jacket from his arms, winds it in a ball, and hurls it at Arvo. Repeating a high school habit to remove any debris gathered on the soles of his shoes, he shakes each leg twice. His stomach quivers at the sight of the other runners' flamboyant spikes. He realizes how much the running world has changed and curses for having tossed the ten on the table.

Carl, a runner with neatly parted hair, squats to rub stray bits of grass from emerald-coloured shoes. The female starter says softly to Carl, "Have a good one."

Carl doesn't crack his mask-like face.

While the starter awaits verification that the timers and judges are in place, Gavin shivers and is reminded of his earlier racing experiences. Three years ago he reigned as North Bay's 1,500-metre champion. That was before his dad's crashed Cessna, on the opening day of the Walleye season, ended his running.

At the pistol crack, Gavin spurts to the front as he had in past years. On the bend his gasping cautions him to relinquish the lead. On the back straightaway he can't hold back and bursts to the fore. The first lap, he has twenty metres on everyone. He flashes bystander Arvo an impish grin. The second time around, still ahead, he has a haunted look like a man summoned to the gallows. His shoulders hunch, and his arms pivot in short arcs like an inebriated disco dancer. Gavin's once free-flowing strides shorten to a waddle similar to a lady in a tight skirt sprinting for a bus.

Carl barks, "Track," as he bolts by Gavin.

"Four minutes flat," a timer calls, when Gavin completes his third lap. Gavin's jaw tightens; his molars grind, and his aquamarine eyes look as pallid as those in a dead pike.

"Hell, I could walk faster than that," Scott murmurs to Arvo. Scott's smirk vanishes when Gavin lurches into a sprint the last 200 metres. "God!" Scott says, looking at his watch, "he might make it! Yes, he's under five." Scott reads, "4:57.33."

Once Gavin crosses the finish, Arvo and Scott stare at Gavin's arms as they flail the air like the sails on a badly tacked boat.

Carl, his hair still neatly parted, jogs by Gavin and says, "I wish you tourists would keep the hell off the track. You screw up the pace."

"Forget it Carl," the shrill voice of coach Andy Tanner rings out. Carl retreats like a scolded puppy.

When Gavin turns, he sees the university coach approach. Gavin notices the coach's lips purse before he asks, "Why not come out with the team? You could do well if you got in some systematic training."

Gavin, tired and confused, says, "I think not, I went in on a bet; I haven't done serious running for years."

"Well you were competitive for almost three laps. Think about it." Tanner waits. When Gavin doesn't respond, the coach directs his attention to the women's 800-metres.

Gavin ponders: At twenty, most athletes have already established themselves; it could be too late to start serious training. What's there to lose. Hanging out with the gang, snapping partridge on the fly, and claiming a day's walleye limit, has been fun, but surely there's more. Besides, training could be a break from studying.

Moments later Scott and Arvo cross the track to where Gavin is kneeling. "You son-of-a-bitch, you did it in spite of your toddle," Scott says.

Gavin pockets the bills Arvo hands him, smiles, and says, "Tanner asked me out for the team." Scott and Arvo lift their heads together.

Scott then asks, "How about it?"

Gavin says, "Maybe I will," with a flicker of amusement in his eyes." Gavin slips his Widdifield jacket over his shoulders, ties the arms in a loose knot, and jogs toward the locker room. The air flushing his lungs has the same tranquilizing effect as slow moving water at the base of steep rapids. He glances at the receding sun and reflects again about Tanner's invitation. Why not! he says to himself and sprints across the final thirty metres of the sports field.

After a shower, he gingerly dries around his blistered toes. In doing so, he brushes a piece of shrapnel dangling on a gold chain from his neck. Gavin smiles at the thought of how he asked his granddad why he kept this piece of steel on his desk. Granddad, a bombardier during the Second World War, recounted how he bailed out of a flaming Mitchell and picked up this souvenir on the way down. Gavin ponders if running could ignite in himself half the excitement his granddad experienced overseas.

Six months ago, a chance comment by a gas bar client made Gavin aware of an academic program in Adventure Leadership at Laurentian University. His application was accepted, and now he has another opportunity to be a runner.

Next morning Gavin grins at the sight of the crumpled bills on the dresser. The mirth sours when he remembers how he was trounced every time he raced outside of North Bay. He considers whether those out-of-town hot shots were that talented after all. At first practice, while waiting to be issued a special team locker, he reflects on how summer guiding for his dad had taken precedence over his high school coach's plea to compete with a club. At that time, frying clients' walleyes over crackling fires on shore lunches was tough to beat. Would training make a whopping difference? He would soon see.

Gavin brushes a moist forehead with the back of his wrist as he leaves the sports complex. He reports to Tanner who is timing runners doing interval training.

When Tanner smiles, Gavin asks, "What would you suggest?

"Start by running down South Bay Road and turn when you've been out twenty minutes. Report back if you have any concerns. Keep the pace even."

The first week it took all Gavin's concentration to not run too fast going out. In his third week, Tanner's instructions include a day of interval training. Gavin ignores irritated shins and tender ankles, but he finally reports a sore knee. Tanner advises him to cut his speed. Soon the pain changes to stiffness.

The last day of September a trial run of four minutes 14 seconds for 1,500-metres earns Gavin a place on the team for the forthcoming Queens University Invitational in Kingston.

Chapter 2

The drone of the University van heading south gives Gavin a dream-like mood. On crossing the French River, he muses how diminutive men guided fur-laden vessels through rocky channels of swirling waters. Wimps don't carry mammoth canoes over tortuous paths or move bulky pelts with paddle-weary shoulders. The task of overcoming the wind, the rain, the frost, the pestering insects, and the unrelenting summer sun makes training for racing a joke. Unless of course, one puts everything one has into the running.

He reflects on how his father's outfitting business flourished until timber cutting opened too many public access roads. Next, exploratory drilling in freshly staked mineral deposits discouraged all but the exclusive fly-in clients. At that time, short on cash, his dad ignored the maintenance schedule on his Cessna once too often. In a confusing world, something as straightforward as running could be his thing.

Shot putter Scott looks up from his magazine, *Your Physique*, and nudges Gavin saying, "What's on your mind?"

"Ah—wonder what it would have been like being a voyageur, sleeping under rock overhangs and all?"

Scott mumbles, "I wouldn't want any part of it," and snaps to the next page.

Gavin's chin drops. An hour later, Gavin notices the autumn sun casting a golden path over the rippling waters of a passing lake. Bordering the rocky shoreline, octopus-like roots crawl out of granite fractures and coalesce into massive pine trunks. How these roots suck sufficient moisture from the rock baffles him.

One towering pine stands out. With branches totally severed on one side it still flourishes. It does what it can with what it has; why can't he do the same?

After pulling in at the Manor Motel in Kingston, the several athletes amble to their rooms. Scott and Gavin drop their bags and flop on beds. In a few minutes Scott scans the television channels and decides, "Not much on the tube."

"Just as well," Gavin replies, "I'm tired from an English assignment I finished last night." Gavin slips off his Adidas flats, stretches out and closes his eyes.

Scott thumbs through the latest *Sports Illustrated.*

A ring snaps Gavin out of a nap. He greets the caller and hears, "Hi, is Scott Cassidy in?" Gavin covers the speaker and says, "Scott, some sweet thing wants to talk with you."

"Scott, it's Sally McCallum from Windsor. The Queen's Coach told me where you were staying."

"Great, glad to hear from you, Sally. I didn't know you were going to Queens."

"Yeah, I'm in physiotherapy. I know you've a meet tomorrow but if you wanted to come over for coffee you could take any bus east and get off at Bagot Street; we're at 241. I'd love to see you. Six of us from Windsor are renting a home. Bring a friend, if you like; my cousin's down from Ottawa."

"Just a moment, I'll check." Scott covers the microphone with his paw and asks, "Hey Gavin this chick from my old high school is inviting a couple of us over. You interested?"

"No chance, I'm tired, want to take it easy tonight."

"Oh, come on, we'll be back early, could be a bit of fun," and a dreamy smile crosses Scott's lips.

"Okay, but no matter what, I'm leaving at midnight."

After taking quick showers and stretching into fresh shirts, the boys are out on Princess Street. Scott hails a cab rather than wait for the unfamiliar bus.

Lanky Sally, with her hazel eyes sparkling, responds to Scott's knock, "Meet my cousin Cynthia," Sally says.

A brunet, with thin lips and a dainty *retroussé* nose says, "Hi," and leans forward to shake hands.

"How about we check the watering hole on Brock Street? It looked lively as we passed," Scott says.

"That's the Pretzel Belle, the footballers' hangout," Sally says.

They retrace the taxi route to the site. Sally points to an unoccupied table in the heart of the boisterousness.

Scott, with his ninety-kilogram mass and natty sports shirt resembles a Blue's footballer as he shuffles toward the raucous Queens fans celebrating the afternoon's victory over Toronto.

When the table talk focuses exclusively on the Windsor happenings, Gavin catches Cynthia's eye and angles his head toward the dance floor. Cynthia nods with a smile.

Gavin and Cynthia frolic to a good beat when suddenly they hear a grating of chairs back at their table.

Gavin notices Scott castigating a burly, curly-haired student wearing a Queens Engineering jacket.

"One thing," Gavin says, when he observes Cynthia's distress, "Scott can look after himself." Cynthia drops her arms and frowns even more at that comment but her legs keep the rest of her supple body magnetized to the rhythm. After three more selections, Cynthia leans on Gavin's shoulder and says, "Let's take a breather."

Gavin delays, hoping the next selection will be a slow one, but it isn't. He guides her to the stand-up bar rather than risk chilling the glowing spark they share by joining the others.

"What brings you to Kingston?" Gavin asks.

"I'm a student at the University of Ottawa and reporting the field hockey tournament for the student newspaper as well as participating."

"Have you taken any specific training for writing?"

"Not really, the sports editor liked my first work and has used everything I submitted since. What events do you do in track?" Cynthia asks.

"Middle distances …"

A quick shuffle of feet and slapping sounds command their attention. A hush descends at Scott and Sally's table. People immediately huddle around Scott.

"Not Scott again," Gavin says. They rush over.

"Le' me go, le' me at the bastard," the same burly student shouts at two people barring his access to Scott. Blood seeps from a gash over the Queens student's eye.

A prolonged moan from Cynthia reddens Gavin's face. Gavin quickly threads his way through the bystanders, grabs Scott's sweat-moistened shirt at the shoulders, pivots him to face the entrance, and with braced elbows rushes Scott through the path cleared by the bouncer. The petrified girls follow.

Outside the Pretzel Belle, Scott says in response to Gavin's scowl, "The twit splashed beer on me."

Ten metres behind, Sally sighs on confiding to Cynthia, "It's incredible, Scott was top all-round student at Glendale Collegiate and quite a pianist."

Sally notices Gavin's over-the-shoulder scan of concern. She calls, "It's okay, we'll get back on our own."

Cynthia doesn't respond to Gavin's goodnight wave.

Gavin shrugs uneasily when he notices a welt forming on Scott's left cheek. The cut on his lip slurs his speech. Gavin hails a cab.

The moment Gavin pays the driver, a runner eases up in the Manor Motel driveway. In the glare from the neon lights, they notice it's coach Andy Tanner. When their eyes meet, Gavin says, "Have a good run Mr. Tanner?" Scott simultaneously drapes his arm across his face feigning scratching his left ear.

"Not bad thanks," Tanner replies with raised eyebrows while he completes a couple of stretches of each calf muscle.

Gavin's stomach sours under Tanner's glare.

"Good night," Tanner finally says.

"Good night," the athletes reply together, with silent sighs.

Gavin watches Scott locate the room's plastic garment bag, leave to fetch ice cubes, and then tie the cubes off in a corner to make a cold compress. Scott's familiarity with this procedure puzzles Gavin. During the night, Scott's shenanigans hound Gavin's slumber.

At the stadium the next day Gavin tests his spikes on the unfamiliar surface before the track competition. When satisfied, he watches Scott compete. He sees a cool, aggressive competitor in no way affected by his previous evening's adventure.

Gavin's legs feel heavy during his warmup; he blames being in the sun too long. Then he wonders if Scott's behaviour last night was getting to him. Why when he needed to be on fire does he feel so bushed? He debates scratching, but fears Tanner would drop him, especially after spotting him returning late. Instead, Gavin trashes his earlier resolve of attempting 67 second laps and settles for a goal two seconds slower. However, for the first three circuits in this ten-athlete race, he hangs on as intended. With a drunken-like weave up the homestretch, he passes two Military College athletes who had started their final kicks too soon. Gavin claims fifth place. He tingles when Tanner tells him his time is 4:08. His bellowing chest, however, rasps like a plumber's saw cutting through copper pipe. A few minutes later, Tanner asks, "How you feeling?"

"Sick, but happy with the time."

"With three more weeks preparation, you could crack the top eight at the Ontario's. They're in Sudbury this year."

With Tanner's words, Gavin floats around feeling little effect of the race; he speculates whether he has underestimated his capability. A sudden jackknifing of his body into a series of croupy coughs reminds him of how far he still has to go.

The loudspeaker's blare conveys the results of the men's shot put, "… And in first place, Scott Cassidy from Laurentian University, with a put of 13.90 metres."

"All right," Gavin shouts, throwing both arms high. When his head clears and his chest stops grating, he scans the bleachers for Scott. However, the 3,000-metre steeplechase has started. Gavin watches in amazement and reflects how stilted the competitors are in coping with the obstacles. Having hustled over many a tree cluttered trail and hurdled umpteen creeks, he spots his pot of gold. I'll talk to Tanner about this event, he decides with a smile, and punches his fist into his open hand.

Gavin finally notices Scott high in the stadium surrounded by two girls. He climbs thinking there must be something about Scott that fascinates females. Immediately he sees Sally; it takes him a further flight to identify Tanya. Tanya, his teammate, is sporting a new Diodora sweat suit; she looks ravishing with the sun glistening on her flushed post-race face.

Gavin immediately slaps Scott's back and says, "Neat-oh!" When he greets Sally the sight of her sagging chin arrests Gavin's mirth. He asks, "Did you hear anything more about last night?"

"Not directly, but the rumour is no one's pressing charges."

The tremor rippling through Scott's face, after Sally's comment, leaves the others frowning. Finally, Gavin says, "You did all right for your first crack with the sixteen pounder."

"Yeah, it wasn't that different from the high school twelve. Perhaps a fraction slower crossing the circle."

All scan the surrounding empty seats in silence. Finally, Gavin stands and says, "I'm dry, would anyone care for a coffee or pop?"

No one responds, and Gavin turns to leave.

"Hold on, I'll join you," Tanya says; she stands and flings her white Puma bag over her shoulder.

As they descend the many steps Tanya remarks, "I wish I'd been in the 3,000-metres today, it didn't look fast."

"Tanner is seasoning you with the shorter stuff before you move up."

"Maybe, but those girls were hardly moving."

Gavin doesn't respond to Tanya's comment. He is grinning in anticipation of his new event. How many years, he asks himself, has he spent scissoring through underbrush, straddling creeks, and belly rolling over deadfalls?

Chapter 3

Starting next workout, Gavin says, "Mr. Tanner, I would like to try that steeplechase they were doing in Kingston."

"That what!" Tanner replies still staring at his stopwatch.

"The steeplechase."

Tanner signals the next runners to start and says, "My God man you're just getting a clue in the 1,500-metres and you want to try the steeplechase? That event's tough; you need the resilience of an Olympic gymnast and the endurance of a marathoner. Landing from the water jump jars hell out of experienced runners. You don't have the background."

"But Mr. Tanner I feel I can handle it, after all, I grew up hiking through all kinds of bush often carrying hunks of moose meat. The steeplechase is perfect for guys like me, not those city robots who never gained the knack for clearing obstacles."

Tanner keeps a solemn face wondering about this cocky kid but admits he makes a strong argument. Besides, he showed resilience running a personal best after being out on the town.

"Well," Tanner says, drawing out the word. "I'll go over the main points; if you can handle the barriers in a trial on Friday, I'll enter you." Tanner slips off his stopwatch lanyard, limbers up his calf muscles, and carries a solid bench to the infield. He then says to Gavin, "Straddle this bench and keep it from moving."

Using an eight metre run Tanner curls his right toe over the far edge of the bench, straightens his knee violently and stretches far out from the bench. When Gavin imitates this action successfully, Tanner drags a steeplechase barrier to the infield. He now demonstrates from the official three-foot height but lands on grass instead of the regular water trough. Tanner smiles as he snares his head back into the lanyard, proud he can still demonstrate the technique he used competing in this event for Canada some years ago.

On the other side of the track Tanya breathes heavily and walks nimbly after having completed her assignment of three 600-metre repeats. She crosses the infield where Tanner and Gavin have been working.

"Mr. Tanner," she says, when he glances her way, "I would like to run the 3,000-metres in the Championships."

"You're not ready, Tanya. You can't handle a sufficient number of repeats. Your speed, on the other hand, is excellent. Focus on the 800 or at most the 1,500-metres until your stamina catches up." Tanya turns away with droopy eyes.

Seeing this, Tanner reconsiders and says, "If you're that serious we can arrange a trial Friday and decide then."

Tanya jogs off beaming and impatient for her trial.

On Friday, Tanya fades badly on the last two laps. Tanner says, "Tanya your projected time for the full distance is five seconds slower than eighth place last year and you'll have already raced the 800. I think you should leave it."

"But Mr. Tanner I've nothing to lose. I'll run as hard as I can in the 800 and then take a crack at the 3,000; it's three hours later."

"Oh—all right," Tanner says but shakes his head negatively.

"Great, Mr. Tanner." Tanya jumps, claps her hands, and skips away like a girl on her tenth birthday.

During the steeplechase trial the moment Gavin enters the last lap Scott shouts, "Hang tough." After Gavin finishes Scott rushes over and says, "Way to go, look at the coach checking his watch."

They both turn to see Tanner shrug his shoulders, scratch his droopy mustache, and raise the peak of his cap to reveal sparkling brown eyes.

On Thursday evening, before the Championship weekend, Gavin and Scott join the student trend and head for the pub. Gavin stops abruptly and points to a bulletin board, "Look at that, an advertisement on the track meet."

Scott smiles while reading and says, "A good crowd might help me unload a big one. Being ranked this early could increase my chances of making the Ontario Team for the Canada Games next summer."

Gavin listens eagerly and realizes in spite of Scott's impatience in day-to-day matters he aims for long-range goals. While finishing his first draft, Gavin spots Tanya standing three tables over. She exchanges words with two male students, her flaxen hair framing the high cheekbones of her smiling face.

A girl Gavin has seen at practice but whose name escapes him accompanies Tanya. Wearing purple cords and a black v-neck sweater, she is of medium height, has mousy brown hair, an oval face, and wears glasses which constantly slide down her nose.

"It's okay Scott, I'll get the next round," Gavin says after Scott attempts to free the back of his chair from the one abutting his. Gavin coughs his way through the smoke to the bar. When Gavin returns, he finds Scott has mustered two chairs for Tanya and her friend who have joined.

"Could I get you girls something?" Gavin asks.

"Sure I'll have a draft," Tanya says.

Tanya's friend gives the slightest negative rotation of her head.

Tanya accepts Gavin's drink with a smile and Gavin fetches another. When Gavin returns, he hears Tanya say, "I'm sure I'll be up for the race Saturday even though I didn't do well in the trial."

Gavin gags and places his drink back on the table. He gazes at Tanya and asks himself, where does her confidence come from?

One of the students Tanya had previously talked with calls over, "Tanya, the guys on third floor, B section are starting their shindig, you still interested?"

Scott, who was in a tête-à-tête with Tanya at that moment, replies, "Sounds good." Scott takes two strides, twists back to ask Gavin, "You comin'?"

"See ya," Gavin says and offers a sloppy salute, before turning his attention to Tanya's friend.

She is frowning at Tanya's abandoned draft. When their eyes meet, she asks, "You in Human Kinetics?"

"Yep, first year—have you known Tanya long?"

"She lives across the hall. When I heard her talking about running, I asked about the team. She's a good runner?"

"She's coming along."

"I enjoy running on roads back home where I plant trees but I've never raced. Tanya told me about the team, so I've been running with her a bit."

"Are you trying out?"

"I thought about it but Tanya said it's tough; I don't think I'm good enough." She blushes and continues, "I couldn't handle that fast stuff."

"Wait a minute," Gavin says.

"Anyways, I'll think about it," she replies, grasps Gavin's hand, and leads him onto the dance floor.

Next morning at swim class, Gavin learns the girl's name is Lisa Charbonneau.

Chapter 4

Friday afternoon Gavin meets Carl on his way to the athletic complex. Above them, a brisk wind chases three days of rain clouds revealing a pale sun.

"Jeez, I hate to run in wet shoes," Gavin mumbles in the dressing room. His fresh socks have sucked in the shoes' dampness.

"Never have trouble with New Balance," Carl says, when he stretches his calves while leaning against the wall.

Gavin muses, if you only train on sunny days you won't have trouble with wet shoes.

They leave the dressing room together and head into a strong wind toward the university beach trail. "My God!" Carl shouts, when he sees the sector tapes for the shot put blown into a tangle. "I guess the time I spent helping Tanner set those tapes is all for naught."

Gavin's attention, however, is on a couple of athletes who have removed McMaster University sweats and now do flawless water jump clearances. Gavin considers he has underestimated his opposition.

"Forget them! Let's go!" Carl says, and spurts ahead. Gavin swallows hard and puts in a burst to catch Carl. As soon as Gavin approaches, Carl accelerates. The same thing happens again, and again. Tanner has cautioned Gavin to run easily the day before his race, but Gavin fears Carl will think him gutless if he doesn't keep up.

When Carl accelerates a fourth time, Gavin calls, "See you Carl, that's it for me."

"But we've only started. You've got to train fast to race well."

"Yes Carl, but not the day before the championships."

Doubts immediately mount in Gavin's mind while he jogs toward the dressing room. He doesn't think quitting is the best thing either, so he adds thirty minutes of controlled running on another trail.

In bed that evening, the sounds from wind buffeting the window harass his sleep. He awakes jerking his right leg into the blankets in an effort to escape the barrier he dreamt he would hit. He sees 6:05 flash on his clock radio. Too early to get up, he decides, but it's also no use lying here either. He pulls the light string and resumes reading *East of Eden*. His stomach growls so he makes tea. Next, he butters bread and smothers it with peanut butter. He wraps it like a hot dog and chews at it. Suddenly, he abandons his food to check the spike length of his competitive shoes. They're too short to grip the water barrier in the push-off he figures. He puts on his racing shorts—too restricted? He cuts the outer seam slit four centimetres with a scissors and remembers to trim his competitor's number. He had watched Carl do this in Kingston to prevent the wind catching its margins. On returning to bed, he notices it is only 7:20 a.m.

"No use losing your control with worry," he remembers Tanner saying. Gavin chuckles at how easy it sounds. He recalls jokes he shared with his dad about clients. A Mr. Proctor, a noted Toronto criminal lawyer, could hit the ace of spades in a sand pit at one hundred metres, but seeing game, he could never steady a shaking rifle. A banker from Columbus, Ohio, who bragged about how experienced a woodsman he was, lost his bearings the moment the bush obscured the shoreline. The loan's officer didn't remember whether the red or silver needle pointed north and couldn't sort out the difference even on a sunny day. Gavin smiles with a long exhaling breath.

A shiver ripples through his shoulders. He knows now what Scott means when he says the heating in residence lags twenty-four hours behind the weather. The thought of wading through ice water in the steeplechase trough makes him wish he had stayed with the 1,500-metres.

He stares at the ceiling reflecting on his adventures as a youngster: playing follow the leader around the upper struts of wire free hydro-towers, cliff jumping into water, and crossing lakes with five centimetre ice thickness clutching cedar poles. No matter, he had survived. Seven laps of the track each having one water jump and four barriers all set at the three-foot height, can't be that tough.

Tanner's assurance that if he could maintain the pace he achieved in the trial, he would be in the top six, encourages him. At nine-thirty Gavin leaves his room. He wears double sweatsuits. He stops for Tanya in the Lobby of University College Residence.

Tanya casually waits, her unzipped, sky blue shell covering her Laurentian sweatsuit. She glows like a child.

"While I'm questioning the value of facing the misery of competing in this weather you don't give it a second thought," Gavin says smiling.

"I had some concern, but once I decided the conditions are equal for all, I stopped worrying."

After walking to the corner of Voyageur Drive, they turn into a raw wind.

"It's not the weather I associate with track meets," Gavin says.

"No. It's only the Ontario Universities who have outdoor competitions in the fall, otherwise there wouldn't be any outdoor track for us at all."

When they reach the sports field a crisp voice over the public address system announces, "Competitors in the 10,000-metres please report." Gavin's heart accelerates for it is the event preceding his.

Forty-five minutes later, the last call for the 3,000-metre steeplechase crackles through the frosty air.

Before Gavin removes his sweats, Tanner touches his shoulder and says, "Anything you do in your first attempt at this event is a bonus."

Gavin, at the crack of the pistol, is caught daydreaming. Sensing the tempo is too fast Gavin hangs back and concentrates on getting a clearer view of each barrier. With one lap completed, five clustered athletes lead a trailing pack of six. Running smoothly and hurdling better than he ever has in practice, Gavin moves through this trailing group. With two laps remaining, it takes him double the effort to negotiate each barrier. He steps on some when he misjudges his lead up steps, even though Tanner's words, "Stepping means raising your centre of gravity too high" hound him. On the second last water jump, a forced shuffle of strides kills Gavin's momentum. He wets his right leg as well as his left in the landing trough. Water now oozes from both shoes and each sock slips on push off.

Gavin concentrates on three stragglers from the elite group. At the bell, he locks his gaze on a blue-clad athlete whose lead leg sways laterally in front of each obstacle. Suddenly, with the enthusiasm of a long lost hunter who discovers his way, Gavin spurts by a tall runner on the backstretch and two clumsy McMaster athletes at the water jump. Where's that impeccable style you guys had yesterday? Gavin chortles to himself. He cruises into third place with a 9 minute, thirty-three second time.

Gavin savours his success through a short warmdown before heading for the shot competition. He sees Scott glare at the ground, grab his sweats, and walk-off.

Gavin asks Arvo, "What happened?"

"Although Scott led after the first three throws, two University of Toronto putters edged him back to third on the final three."

Gavin missed Tanya's 800-metre during his race recovery. He now observers her lined up on the far side of the track waiting for the 3,000-metre start. Gavin watches Tanner beside him start his watch with the flash of the pistol. The coach then fills out relay personnel declaration forms in between timing Tanya's laps. When Tanya starts passing runner after runner on the home stretch, Tanner drops his pen, scans his watch, and smiles saying, "What d'you know, she's fourth in under ten minutes."

"What an improvement!" Gavin says.

During the awards ceremony Gavin edges close to Tanya and asks, "There's a party tonight at Lance's place. He's a swimmer and a chap I take physics with who lives close by. Would you care to go?"

Tanya's eyebrows lift, and she says, "Sure."

"About seven?"

"Great!"

Chapter 5

While soaking in a hot bath, Tanya dozes. Waking, she stretches, checks her wristwatch on a side-stool, and creases her brow. She heats a small square of lasagna in the communal kitchen microwave, returns her mother's call to Toronto, sets a few curls, and dabs a bit of eye shadow. She is climbing into black, pull-on pants to go with her grey, knit tunic when Gavin knocks.

Gavin utters, "Hi," shocked that, within an hour, Tanya, the sunken-eyed shivering creature at the awards ceremony, has now such radiating eyes and flushed cheeks.

While Gavin gawks, Tanya says "Don't you look spiffy?"

"Thanks," Gavin replies blushing.

Tanya picks up her handbag, locks the door, and takes two sprightly steps before Gavin says, "It's not far; how about we take a shortcut through the bush?"

Tanya stops, looks at her grey slip-ons with rubber soles and says, "Sure."

They walk up South Bay Road for one minute and Gavin says, "This scraggly pine marks the start of the trail."

The embankment from the road is steep, and Gavin takes a couple of quick steps to gain momentum. He offers Tanya a hand. They use a trail of protruding roots and rocks and bordered with stunted balsam trees. It leads over a ten-centimetre layer of oak leaves at the bottom of a steep hill. Using rocks uncovered by eroded soil as solid footholds, they climb. Faded blueberry plants border the passageway. Gavin leads Tanya on a side path to a rock ledge overlooking Bethel Lake. Tanya stumbles, regains balance, and grips Gavin's offered hand. Gulls frolic in swooping power dives below them filling the air with a cacophony of shrieks. In the west, the copper sun glimmers through the tree line.

Their eyes drift from the horizon to each others. Gavin hugs Tanya as though they had both climbed Mount Everest. A squirrel romping at Tanya's feet startles her. They chuckle and return to the main path.

Several cars crowd Lance's driveway. It is situated half way down a long descent of the street. On his lawn, a dozen well-spaced spruce trees provide privacy. The back yard eases down to the lake. They mount the front steps and add their shoes to the assortment at the door. With the ruckus inside, Gavin gives a token knock and enters.

Tanya notices how the hallway opens into three tiers: the kitchen to the immediate south, the dining room a twenty centimeters drop to the north, and a five step descent to a crowded room with a pool table to the east.

Gavin puzzles over people scampering and shouting around the pool table without using pool cues. He leads Tanya a couple of steps toward the table, but stops when he notices Alex Baumann on the lakeside north balcony. Baumann and Arvo are filling their steins from a beer ball.

"Glad you could make it," Gavin hears behind him. On turning he waves with a grin at Lance who adds, "Grab a draft, we'll be starting the next game of Thunder Bay Pool in a minute."

"Thanks," Gavin replies, but he is anxious to eavesdrop on Arvo and Alex. He edges his way onto the balcony. Tanya joins others standing on the carpeted seat by the pool table. Arvo and Alex exchange jokes, until Arvo notices Gavin beside him. Arvo lowers his draft and asks, "Alex, what contributes most to your swimming success?"

Baumann smiles at Arvo's bluntness and scratches his chin before saying, "Training at six most mornings and then again at four in the afternoons is vital. A swimmer also has to be on the right program depending on what he's aiming for. Once he gets in the strengthening and conditioning he has to get it out of himself at the right time." Baumann stops for a moment, licks his lips, discreetly and with a devilish smile continues, "It's flat out in competition no matter how you feel. You can't say, I've a headache or a sore back; you're always hurting. Once you decide you can manage the pain you forget about it. Olympics don't wait for injuries to go away." Alex shrugs and looks up at soaring gulls.

"Have you special talent that gives you an inside edge?" Arvo asks.

"Perhaps, but it's what you do with what you have that counts. Most everyone has something he's good at—.

"Why draw blood, since when is a good effort not enough?" Carl interjects from his position beside Gavin. Baumann lowers his gaze and smiles.

Arvo's eyes bulge and his lower lip quivers, "Carl, if I wanted your opinion I would have asked for it."

Carl persists, "Having an obsession stultifies your normal life."

Arvo, a graduate anthropologist, jerks his head and stares at Carl, "What's normal? What most people do? That's average. That's typical, but it's not normal. What's normal for man since he roamed this earth is a physically vicious lifestyle. Successful mutations forged man's body to cope with heavy physical demands. Modern man's recent inactivity is out of step with his evolutionary success."

A hush descends on the pool game. All eyes focus on a sheepish Arvo who blushes while he returns to softly pumping the draft ball. Once the pool game resumes, Baumann says to Carl, "If you, a university student, can't appreciate perfection that's your problem." Baumann turns and his eyes meet Gavin's anxious look.

Gavin asks in a polite tone, "How many personal pleasures do you have to give up to be great?"

Baumann gives Gavin an avuncular smile and says, "Within reason, not a lot. You have to make sure your staying up late doesn't interfere with practice. You train no matter how you feel; with experience you get your sleep and cut your suds or anything else that sabotages your training. The crucial thing's the daily demanding activity that you have slowly increased in quantity and or quality."

"Don't you get sick of going up and down the pool?" Carl asks in a subdued voice.

Baumann looks at Carl with a frown, sighs and then grins, "You do but that's what it's all about. A musician gets drained perfecting the same piece the same as a hockey player with skating and shooting." Baumann pauses, rubs his chin again and adds, "Of course we do weight training, cycling and some running as diversions but stroke work is the key. Excuse me please." Baumann lifts a mock toast with his half empty glass and drifts to the pool table.

Ouch! A tipsy brunette screeches on stubbing her toe on the stair's top projection. A friend of the injured girl snaps a flash when Baumann shows concern for her injury.

Tanya grips Gavin's shirt and tugs him over to the action on the pool table. "They're starting a new game. The object is to sink the moving red ball with the white. It's my turn. Watch!" Tanya grabs the white, rushes to the nearest end of the pool table and lines up the red with her white. She hits the red but it doesn't go in a pocket. "Grab the white ball Gavin and move to the end. That's it."

During lulls in the game, Gavin tries to sort out Baumann's points on being an athlete. Gavin still doesn't know how to tell if he has sufficient talent to do well, but from the discussion he figures no one else starting out ever knows either.

Next day, Gavin is towelling himself in his residence after an eight-kilometre run when Scott asks, "Could you hand in my psych paper tomorrow? I've a dental appointment."

Gavin whips the back of his hand to his forehead and sighs; he has forgotten about the assignment. "Sure Scott."

Gavin figures there has to be a catch to all the university fun. Would he flunk out through carelessness? Maybe he doesn't belong, none of his relatives have ever gone to university. He could sense his progress for instructors' vocabularies no longer intimidated him but forgetting a major assignment was not good.

Although he read extensively for this paper, he took only scant notes. His topic revolved around human motivation.

Baffled by details, he never could sort out where to start. After hours of frustration, he decides to visit Tanya.

He finds her door ajar. He knocks and enters diffidently. The setting sun silhouettes Tanya as she works by the window. She is typing frantically trying to capture a fleeting thought.

She stops when Gavin coughs, swivels sideways, stands, and says, "Hi there." Noticing his drawn features and file folder, she asks, "Having problems?"

"Well, yes," Gavin says staring innocently at her. But at that moment she has doubled his torment. Seeing her as a serious student has further cast her out of his sphere. Did her elegance, he wonders, come from growing up in an affluent home or was it the glow of achievement?

When she walks toward him, he wants to hug her but instead blurts, "What y'a working so seriously on?"

When Tanya glares back with a question mark, he wishes he could retract his comment. Lacking a lightning retort, Gavin buries his head and thoughts in his folder.

With Tanya's help, he clears another obstacle on his academic trail but resolves nothing about his feelings for her.

Chapter 6

Next morning as Gavin pokes the alarm button on his clock radio he notices the date: 18 October. He smiles since it is his birthday, and he remembers celebrating these weekends with his dad guiding moose hunters.

Peeking through the east window, he sees how the sun's rays electrify the hoarfrost on the nearby spruce boughs. He recalls similar scenes sitting in a tree hide calling, while a client waited anxiously.

With the track team on a week of informal workouts following the outdoor championships, Gavin plans double training sessions today. The tangle in his mind over Tanya sidetracks him. He crawls back under the blankets; tomorrow, he assures himself, will be soon enough. After all, the next competition isn't until December. An hour passes while he debates his chances with Tanya; she may be friendly but she would never get involved with a bushwhacker, he concludes.

When he gets up to put water to boil, he hears Arvo showering after his morning roller skiing session. The vibrating soft palate of Arvo's roommate echoes from the room walls. Gavin glances at his watch: 9:20; the chemistry class at 9:30 will be too much of a rush. He decides to again borrow Tanya's notes. The professor goes too fast anyway, he figures. He savours his hot chocolate. However, guilt swamps his every thought. When Arvo passes his room again with a towel around his waist; he resolves to train between his psychology and aquatic classes. Gavin makes the psychology class and hands in the assignments. He returns to his room for a ten-minute nap before running. Ten minutes extends to an hour. Finally, he grasps his bathing suit and rushes to the pool reassuring himself that he will get in a longer workout after classes. Though a swimmer, Gavin's crude strokes earn him a novice group assignment. Lisa is a beginner. Tanya, a former competitive swimmer, frequently assists the instructor. Gavin dislikes the chlorination and shivers every time he leaves the water.

After aquatics class he heads for the cafeteria with Tanya and Lisa. Lisa drops a running flat from her paraphernalia as she squeezes through a doorway.

"Why did you bring your running things?" Tanya asks.

"I went for a short run after my psych class; you know how Tanner suggested we break our training into two sessions."

"Yeah! Good, good," Tanya replies and adds, "I'm taking the week off, need a break."

Gavin turns and stares at Tanya; not following the coach's recommendation was one thing, advertising it was something else.

After lunch Gavin returns to his room and picks up his current paperback *East of Eden.* He was reading where Lee describes his belief in the interpretation, "Thou mayest." There is a choice; nothing is predetermined? A ringing telephone interrupts his meditation.

"'Ello—Gavin, it's your Uncle Jacques, *ça va?*"

"Hi Jacques, good to hear from you."

"'Appy Birthday. 'Ow's the student? Soft life eh! Ha, ha."

"It's great, I'm out for track, training to be a runner."

"No kiddin'."

"Came third in the Ontario University Championships last Saturday."

"Great, great," Jacques replies and after a pause says, "you know, I was plannin' going North for some moose 'unting with Bill; you remember Bill Turnbull, my neighbour?"
"Sure, sure."

"Well 'is wife, she 'as pneumonia; Bill can't make it."

"That's too bad."

"Yeah, I 've everything organized, food, gear and even the plastic-covered camp with plenty of fire wood; that's the breaks though."

Gavin starts calculating. He knew students cut classes for special and not so special occasions. He replies, "Jacques, if you stop for my rifle and hunting pack and last year's license in my room at *grand'mère's*, I would be happy to join you on Wednesday after class, at about one-thirty."

"No kiddin'!"

"Yes, I can catch up on school when I get back."

"Well that would be fantastic. Sure, I will pick up your things at mother's."

"Yes, wait for me up at the University College Residence parking lot. There's a map when you turn on campus. I'll watch for you."

The moment Gavin puts down the telephone he reaches for his sweatsuit. A nuclear force soars inside of him.

Wednesday, after class, Gavin notices Jacques sitting patiently in his covered pickup. He waves, runs up three flights of stairs, drops his books, and clutches his prepared duffle bag.

"See you," Gavin calls to Scott as he leaves the apartment interrupting Scott's scanning of the October issue of *Ontario Athletics*. Gavin trots briskly through the noontime rush to Jacques' truck. He hops in the truck, ruffles Jacques' shoulder with his two hands and quips, "How the hell are you?"

Jacques finishes stuffing his Sherlock Holmes pipe and scratches a match head into fire with his thumbnail. The smell of Amphora tobacco fills the cab. Jacques removes his pipe as if to say something, places it back and bursts into an infectious grin as he puts the gearshift in reverse.

When Gavin turns to guide Jacques out of a tight parking spot, he notices the aluminium craft with blue longitudinal streaks that belonged to his dad. The last time he was in that boat they salvaged his father's belongings from the crashed Cessna.

Jacques, on driving through Sudbury says, "There's one thing I must tell you. Your Cousin Armand, borrowed your 300 Savage; I brought my spare .303 for you."

Gavin frowns and wants to ask what right Armand had to do that? Instead, he mumbles, "It's okay."

Jacques, a fifty-year-old bachelor, has bald areas in front and back and an irregular smudge of shortly cropped hair in between. A neatly trimmed, greyish-flecked beard outlines his jaw. Every time the sun breaks through the cloud cover, Gavin detects a mischievous twinkle in Jacques' brown eyes. Jacques lights up fresh Amphora in Chelmsford, while Gavin renews his license at the Canadian Tire Store. As they again swerve north on Highway 144, Gavin climbs into his woollen long johns.

Leaving the boat launch area in Duke Lake, they set off south bucking forty centimetre waves. Within four minutes, a bombardment of hail forces Jacques to cut speed while they twist arms and legs into rain suits.

Five lakes and ten kilometres later the hail stops. Jacques makes a sharp left turn through lily pads onto shore. He ties the boat and pauses to take out a plasticized map. Using his finger he traces their route due east to a cigar shaped lake and says, "Tuck this map somewhere in case you need it." They then shoulder the packs.

"It's a twenty minutes 'ike; we 'ave a canoe in there; I brought it in last summer."

With a 20-kilogram backpack and Jacques' .303 gripped at its balance point, Gavin follows Jacques up the steep, pine needled mountain. Soon the rim of Gavin's orange cap drips with sweat even though it is barely above freezing.

At the top, Jacques scans the trees, focuses on one and whispers, "This way."

Gavin smiles as he passes a spruce tree with a red, plastic ribbon tied around it. While Jacques catches his breath, Gavin notes his Silva compass indicates the trail goes due east.

They cross a gully with a lazy creek and then dodge branches and deadfalls through an aspen grove. Many moose tracks crisscross, but no fresh droppings or recently munched twigs command their attention. Gingerly they mount a moss-covered cap rock.

Jacques, with his one free hand, grips each pine tree branch he can to partially pull himself up the slick surface. On top he pauses and points to tracks resembling a stubby giant human hand with exaggerated curled fingernails, and says, "Seldom see them but they're always around."

In a cluster of hickory scrub, Jacques lifts his free arm and says, *"Voila"*.

Gavin sees a translucent, plastic-covered, pole framed structure. Its roof slants backwards toward a mountain and faces a narrow, kilometre long lake stretching north.

"That lake's not big enough for a plane to land but big enough for us, eh," Jacques says smiling. With quickened strides, Jacques reaches the camp. He pushes the piece of firewood aside that anchors the plastic door. Then using a forked stick, he jams the plastic door open. Jacques enters and slings his pack and rifle on a bunk. Gavin notices the bunks and table have been crafted from chain-sawed planks.

"Quite a camp!" Gavin says while he scans the sections of carpet that cover the earthen floor.

"This I call roof pushups," Jacques says flushing the settled rainwater from the plastic covered roof. He does this by hoisting a board against the carpet that rests over spruce poles spaced thirty-centimetres apart. The carpet provides an underlay for the sheets of plastic. Jacques then goes outside to twist the stovepipes upright and secure them with wire.

Gavin lights birch bark and reaches to the back of the stove to heat the area under the chimney. He adds increasingly larger pieces of wood to the small oil drum stove. Gavin notes how the upper third of the front half of the stove has been replaced with a welded metal plate. This provides a flat cooking area. Some smoke oozes from the home made door's edges until the stovepipes have dried sufficiently and a good draught established.

"We're well, we're well," Jacques says as he packs some Amphora tobacco into his pipe. Gavin pauses between feeding the fire, to get water from the lake. Stepping on three solid rocks, he is able to submerge his blue water container. Air gurgles as the water enters. A yodel-like call echoes from across the lake.

While the kettle heats, they change to dry clothing, blow up air mattresses, and unroll sleeping bags. Jacques pours boiling water for two cups of tea and lights his pipe. He smokes for four minutes. As if remembering something, he returns his metal cup to the stove and pokes behind his bed. He retrieves a funnel-shaped birch bark object held together with friction tape. Jacques puts on his outdoors jacket and cap, slips his rifle sling on his shoulder, and ducks out the door.

In three minutes Gavin hears what a non-hunter would consider a Hereford cow mooing. Jacques returns and blows on his folded wet hands. He grasps his enamel cup from the stove and releases it just as quickly. He utters, "S.T." while he shakes his fingers. Using an old leather glove, he picks it up and places it on an upturned stump. He then relights his pipe from a flaming twig, leans back on his folding chair, and with a gleeful smile says, "Fresh tracks by the creek in the soft muck. We don't have much time before dark but let's check."

Jacques takes out his hunting knife, slices a chunk of cheese, balances it on the blade, and offers it to Gavin. "This should keep you going 'till we make a proper meal."

They snack for two minutes while the smell of pine fills the air. "Let's go," Jacques says and abandons his pipe beneath the stove before gripping his .308 Remington.

Gavin puts a jacket over his doeskin shirt, adjusts his orange peak cap and ducks through the double hanging sheets of plastic that serve as a door. Once outside he slips a clip of shells into his borrowed .303 rifle.

They follow a trail over several fallen aspen and to the upper reaches of a narrow creek. Above them, water cascades from a mountain into three levels of beaver dams. In the other direction by the lake, the shoreline is clear; they find seats on a couple of wind-downed trees. Jacques uses the vertical roots of his as a backrest.

At the creek, Gavin is certain he hears humans talking and turns his head to face the waterfall.

Jacques whispers, "That's only the babblin' brook."

Thirty minutes later, the snapping of branches followed by splashing water has Jacques slowly raising his Remington. Gavin checks his .303 but doesn't work the bolt; they listen for further movement.

Suddenly the forest seems to move; a huge aspen hurtles to the ground; a kerplunk sound in the water follows five seconds later. They exchange smiles and wait in vain for something larger.

Under the glare of the Coleman lantern, Jacques adds cut garlic to a couple of onion embedded steaks. Gavin peels and slices potatoes before easing them into corn oil in another pan. He shifts them until they brown into what Jacques calls silver dollars.

When they crawl into bed two hours later, Gavin notices Jacques unsheathe his hunting knife and places it on a wooden folding chair.

"What's that for?" Gavin asks.

"Bears."

"What in hell will you do with a knife if a bear comes?"

"Slit the plastic and get the 'ell out."

At midnight, a crashing sound like a horse walking in shallow water comes from the creek where the aspen has fallen. Jacques grasps his flashlight from the folding chair while his toes prod the carpet for his slip-ons. His shoulders convulse in the camp's crisp air. He stretches into his orange hunting jacket. "I'll check it," he whispers to Gavin, who was concentrating on the sound's direction.

Jacques stiffens when the night air hits his minimally clad legs. He slips twice creeping over frost to the lake. The chilly air drives him back to camp.

"Couldn't see a thing," Jacques mumbles and heaves a birch over the coals. He readjusts his Wood's Two Star over his air mattress and cuts the flashlight. He pauses at an image of himself dancing on the plastic wall as light slants through cracks in the stove's door.

Gavin can't sleep. Predicting where that moose will be in the morning gives him no respite. He asks himself why moose pop up when least expected and at other times a person could hunt for weeks in vain. Suddenly he sighs, chastising himself at his fervour for hunting. What's happening to my commitment to be a runner, he asks himself? Tanner's words, "You can't wish your way to the top" are reinforced in his mind with the passage in *East of Eden*, "Thou mayest" which Gavin interprets as meaning you can do it if you don't bugger up your time doing trivial things. He thinks of his Uncle who at fifty is still able to hunt, whereas he can only race fast now.

Later, Gavin wakes to the wind slapping the plastic above his head. His back muscles twitch when he curls his toes into Adidas' discards. He grabs a birch log, follows the strip of carpet over the uneven dirt floor to the stove and eases the wood in. He springs back; kicks the stove door closed, and in the process singes his long underwear. On his first step outside, he wishes he had taken time to put on his jacket. Facing downwind, ten paces from camp, he releases his tea-inflated bladder. A glance at the sky and he figures dawn is still a long way off. The ground creaks, as he shuffles back to camp.

Gavin wakes an hour later when a chilly gust sweeps over his face. He sits up and sees Jacques with the door flap open.

Jacques hesitates, closes the plastic flap and anchors it with a log. He then shines the flashlight on his wristwatch, "Just about time" he mumbles.

Within fifteen minutes, the sound of sizzling bacon and the smell of fresh coffee has Gavin climbing into woolen army pants.

Over their second coffee Jacques says, "I think that moose will be over in the aspen grove," he points south of the camp. Gavin agrees to cover the other most likely spot: the creek at the lake's north end.

"Gavin, the wind is quieter but remember that water is cold," Jacques says as he adds a slab of resinous pine stump and closes the stove's draft.

"Don't worry about me Jacques; I grew up in a canoe; I even turned it upright for a flying start this morning."

They linger until Jacques abruptly gets up, pulls the plastic door aside and says, "The sky's brighter, time to boogie."

With a final check of rifle and pack, Jacques cuts the Coleman.

Gavin unties the canoe and grabs a paddle. He frowns at the brightness in the eastern sky and regrets having stayed for a second cup.

"Wait, I'll 'old the canoe for you," Jacques says.

"No problem," Gavin replies. He lowers his small pack and his .303 into the canoe. Then he uses his fingers to clamp his paddle across each side of the craft. When he notices the beaver have left branches floating in the launch area, he gives an extra hearty shove and hops in. His landing foot skids on black ice. He keeps moving; his shoulder crashes into the right gunwale. As the canoe tumbles, Gavin's right arm lunges for the rifle. The cold water forces him to gasp several times making him light headed. He is thankful he has on his personal flotation device. He thrashes with his free arm while his legs cycle frantically. Water slowly trickles through the layers of clothing to his skin.

Gavin feels an infestation of icy spiders crawling over him. He continues his eggbeater like motion until a foot grazes bottom and he can stand. Shivering, he hands Jacques his rifle on shore and then retrieves the canoe, pack, and paddle.

Jacques hauls the canoe up, tips water out, and pushes it upright partially back in the lake. When Gavin plods toward camp, Jacques says, "What's that about growing up in a canoe?" Jacques quakes with laughter as he sparks the Coleman back to life. He dries the .303 with a cloth while Gavin wrings his clothes and hangs them by the fire.

Fifteen minutes later Gavin sets off north wearing an old sweatsuit under dry army pants. He slaps a clip of dried shells into the undercarriage but refrains from bolting a shell into the chamber. Slowly he works his canoe up the lake scouring the mountain for last night's prowler. He paddles through many bark-stripped sticks at the mouth of a creek.

The rising sun glistens from the frost on the dense spruce. It reminds him of Christmas cards years ago so proudly displayed on *grand'mère's* fireplace mantle. On rounding a sharp bend of the creek he pauses with his paddle above the water. A huge greyish boulder protruding above the lilies resembles a moose. Closer inspection assures him it is too big for a moose. Gavin lowers his paddle slowly into the water. When he does, he identifies the boulder as a cow moose thirty-metres up stream, partially hidden by a spruce tree. He missed it earlier, he figured, because it was grazing close to her hind legs. Gavin gently places the paddle in the canoe and discreetly rummages for a free shell in his pocket, rather than risk the noise of jacking a shell into the barrel. Next, he opens the bolt slowly while restricting the shell below from popping up with his left thumb. But as he starts to insert the new shell, his thumb slips and the two cartridges jam. His arms shake in unison with his thumping chest. Swearing, Gavin peers helplessly at the enormous moose.

It was as though the animal could lip-read; for she lifts her head, stiffens her ears and brazenly gallops off prudishly avoiding such abusive language. Moments later, Gavin clears the jam.

In spite of his repeated efforts at imitating a calf and a bull, the cow stays under cover. Attempts at stalking in the alder swamp prove impractical. Gavin continues by walking up stream to a main beaver damn with a large clearing. He remains until two o'clock, returns again in the late afternoon, and each day thereafter, futilely beckoning the cow with different versions of a bull grunt.

On the drive to Sudbury, Gavin complains about his luck. Jacques says, "S.T. you're fortunate to see one at all. They usually don't feed in the creeks as the weather gets colder and we're past the best callin' time."

The site of the university gives Gavin a sinking stomach; within six weeks, he has strayed from his commitment to be a top runner.

Chapter 7

At four-fifteen on Sunday afternoon Gavin limps into residence, climbs to his room, drops his bag on his desk, and collapses on his bed. At ten o'clock that evening, he slips off his clothes and crawls between sheets.

In the morning, his back aches, his legs feel stiff, and he notices puffiness around the knee he twisted while tipping. Wrinkling his forehead, he asks himself, why do I let myself get sidetracked when I want to be a runner? After snacking on peanut-butter-covered toast and hot chocolate, Gavin heads for class. Images of a moose, and a jammed rifle interrupt his concentration.

At five that evening Gavin changes into sweat clothes. When he jogs toward the track, he hears a series of "Ah-ah-ah" cries with deep thuds. Under the floodlights, sporting a heavy black toque, Scott growls like a bear roused from hibernation. He retrieves the shot with his gloved left hand, walks back to the circle, and fires the steel ball with his right. Every slam of his arm comes out quicker than the previous one. Each shot, lost in the black sky, comes back into vision when contrasted with the green grass.

Tanner, wearing a green toque that stretches to his eyebrows and over his ears, smiles when Gavin arrives. While nudging his toque higher on his forehead, Tanner says, "After your warmup, do nine runs of 300-metres, take a 100-metre walk in between each." Tanner pauses to signal Lisa to start her run from across the track. He then places his hand on Gavin's shoulder, and says, "I want you to do quality running as long as the track is free from ice—maybe up to mid-November. Incidentally, if you continue your improvement, you could be in range for next summer's Canada Games. You might consider the Ontario trials in June."

Gavin lifts his eyebrows, flashes his ivories and floats through his warmup. However, his first three repeats are slow and the subsequent three even slower.

Tanner is stone-faced, and wishes he could retract his Canada Games comments. When Gavin hobbles around in his recovery; Tanner intercedes, "Gavin, running at that speed is useless, scrap the last three. See you tomorrow."

Gavin's body still aches; he expected trouble but not this much. He sits on a nearby bench and removes his spikes. On spotting Scott carrying his shot back to the equipment room, he joins him.

Scott says to Gavin, "I can't get any speed across that damn circle in this weather. Those guys in Toronto have it made training indoors; I'll get them though." He lobs his shot from waist height into a wooden storage box. The groaning container emphasizes his point. Scott then smacks the side of his fist into the cinderblock wall.

"Take it easy Scott," Gavin says with a forced chuckle, "don't burn yourself up over those guys."

Scott snarls, "I don't enjoy placing third."

They return to residence in silence. Gavin, rather than face making dinner with the morose Scott, drops in on Tanya.

After exchanging smiles and hugs, Gavin says, "Hey, I didn't see you at practice; did you train earlier?"

"No, my Student Council Meeting didn't finish on time."

"Too bad, that nip in the air made it a great night to train even though I felt lousy."

"I'll run under the street lights before I turn in," Tanya says and adds, "By the way, mother called from Toronto; she mentioned my high school alumni are having their Christmas Holiday Dance; would you care to go?"

Gavin gapes pop-eyed at Tanya, and a grin stretches across his tanned cheeks, "Ah, … I haven't any special plans after Christmas."

"Mother is happy to have you stay at our place. My sister would have a riot meeting you," Tanya's eyes beam.

"Sure! *grand'mère's* place is quiet after Christmas. I've never seen much of Toronto."

Gavin now feels airborne every time he thinks of Tanya. She mustn't have anyone special, he concludes. A twinge of caution crosses his mind remembering how uncomfortable he is in big cities. He spends more time cultivating the cowlick above his forehead. Then he starts bagging his soiled clothes instead of tossing them in the corner of his closet. He even joins Tanya doing laundry on Tuesday evenings for two weeks. When a flash thought convinces him that he is becoming effeminate, he makes a point of not shaving for a week.

With late November winds vibrating the dormant stadium loudspeakers, Tanya, Lisa, and Gavin are the key athletes doing regular laps of the track. In the throwing circle, Scott matches the ferocity of the weather by blasting shot after shot day after day.

A serious snowfall the last week of November chases the middle-distance runners to the Sudbury Arena. They join the sprinters and coach Tanner. The three weekly indoor sessions are at a faster pace than those on the outdoor track, but the workouts are shorter. The other days, Gavin runs for an hour minimum on the shoulders of South Bay Road. Scott uses unscheduled periods in the university gymnasium to put the shot onto older tumbling mats.

In early December, at the University of Western Ontario's first indoor season competition, Gavin chases elite runners over a 200-metre oval and cracks four minutes for the 1,500-metres. Yes, he must be coming along, he figures, for Tanner again smiles broadly at his time.

Following his last exam, Gavin catches a bus home or at least the only place he now calls home: his maternal grandmother's in North Bay. After the liquidation of his parents' assets, *Grand'mère* Vernier insisted Gavin move into her home. Gavin winterized *grand'mère's* attic with fiberglass insulation and finished it with Gyprock. He then called in a friend to help him extend a hot air vent. This has been his base ever since.

Grand'mère Vernier at eighty-one is slightly stooped, but the hint of ageing ends there. Heedless of the one kilometre walk into the business area, she frequents the public library and does her own shopping. Visitors to her home never leave without a game of Scrabble. Her other daughter, Theresa, runs a grocery purchasing service for shut-ins. Her son Armand helps on Saturdays. They live on the second floor of *grand'mère's* home.

Grand'mère was reading her large print book when Gavin came charging in, *"Bonjour Grand'mère."*

"Tu restes pour Nöel?"

"Oui, mais je vais partir après."

"Okay, Okay, *c'est bien.*"

They have tea while *grand'mère* inquires, with some envy, about Gavin's university courses. Her barrage of questions never ceases until she has to leave for her Friday evening bridge game.

On entering his bedroom, the sight of the exposed tape over the gyproc junctions reminds Gavin of his incomplete job. He remembers abandoning the work when his mother informed him she intended staying in the Yukon. He has since regretted the harsh exchange they had. He raises the Venetian blinds and notices steel stanchions projecting out of the snow in the adjacent lot. Thank goodness, he reflects, they are building north of *grand'mère's* garden. His cot is still intact. The 300 Savage, he inherited from his grandfather Goslin, is in his rifle case in the closet.

Alone in the house, Gavin suddenly feels rootless. He calls Pete, his high school buddy, and plans to join the gang at Wylders.

While on their first round Pete, a fair-haired, insurance trainee, says, "They've lots of snow at Mont. St. Antoine, what do you say we get a group together and go skiing?"

Gavin smiles but doesn't reply.

Five jokes later Larry, a short, stocky student from Canadore mentions, "The gang's pickup hockey is at midnight Tuesdays, why don't you join us Gavin?"

Gavin shrugs his shoulders.

"What's the matter, don't you raise a sweat any more?" Pete asks. Then adds,

"What you doin' for excitement?"

"Running."

"Running? Pete inquires, "What do you mean?"

"I'm out for track, doing the steeplechase, clearing a water jump and four other three-foot barriers each lap." Gavin's eyes beam as he talks.

"Don't be a dreamer, you don't have the speed. I could breathe down your neck every 800-metres we ever raced, and I'm slow. If you're going to hack it as a runner you have to have lots of fast-twitch fibers, or run ten kilometres to school every day like the Kenyans."

"We'll see," Gavin replies almost inaudibly. Little did he realize his running ambition was as fragile as a sneeze on a three-dimensional house made of playing cards. The shock of the possibility that he has been kidding himself hits him. He doesn't smile the rest of the evening.

Larry asks, "How are those university babes? I hear they bend for a friend."

Gavin smiles but doesn't react. He is preoccupied with Pete's comment. It's true; there wasn't that much difference in their speed over the 800-metre distance. Gavin scrounges a ride home with the first person to leave. At home, he starts on an intended fifteen-kilometre run but turns back after a lack-luster four. When he showers he tries to confront the reality that he doesn't have blinding speed and that he may be handicapped in his dream of being a middle distance runner. On returning to the kitchen to make a cup of tea, the whiff of garlic reminds him of his Mother and how they had parted so abruptly. This sadness displaces the need for sleep. He remains up until dawn watching late movies on *grand'mère's* black and white set in the semi-finished basement.

As Jacques carves the Christmas turkey at *grand'mère's*, he says, "Gavin, 'ave you being practicin' the one armed dog paddle in ice water lately?"

"No, but I'm sure I could slip a fresh round into the firing chamber of your .303 blindfolded and not disturb the lower cartridge."

Armand's eyes never left the drumstick Jacques had tossed him. A subdued smile circles the table.

In between hands of Hearts, Gavin confirms his bus will arrive in Toronto at the time he has given Tanya. Two days later, he has spring in his stride when he boards the Greyhound.

Chapter 8

At the Bay Street Terminal, Gavin retrieves his vinyl bag with the Royal Bank icon and joins the rush to the main concourse. He scans for Tanya without success, then edges his way outside. A wind, laced with snow, greets his first steps across the sidewalk. While he stares at the southbound traffic, a cabby pulls up. Gavin rotates his head negatively and still the cab stops. A lady, clutching an oversized purse, brushes his shoulder to get in the back door. Gavin shuffles away from the Bay Street curb. While he does so, his gaze climbs the eighteen-storied buildings. He experiences the same queasy feeling he has when an elevator accelerates and his stomach stays behind. Shifting his view west, he notices how the high rises obliterate the feeble, setting sun. When he redirects his attention to street level, he sees Tanya smiling, not ten metres away, locked in traffic. Gavin rushes over, pushes, pulls, and finally opens the cream-coloured, door.

"Well hi," Tanya says extending her hand to give Gavin's arm a squeeze. She brakes and accelerates every ten seconds oblivious to the siren and red flashing lights traveling in the opposite direction. Finally she shifts out of stagnant traffic in a series of turns and makes her way north to Strathearn Boulevard. There she follows a curved driveway lined with sugar maples. Two sentinel looking blue spruce guard the front walkway.

"Just like *grand'mère's*," Gavin chuckles. He swallows hard, gets out of the car and studies the height of the trees. He marvels at their symmetry and how free they are from the ravages of spruce budworm.

"Hi I'm Tanya's mother," he hears behind him. Gavin pivots, still figuring how someone has strung Christmas lights on the spruces' uppermost branches; he shakes the extended hand.

"Make yourselves comfortable. I'm hostess again at the Blood Donor Clinic. See you later."

Mrs.Thoburn drapes her tweed coat over her left arm, unclasps a key, and strides towards a black Mercedes.

Gavin, in his tired-looking ski jacket, grips his vinyl bag and follows Tanya through the main entrance. After squirming out of Adidas flats at the door, he climbs a curved stairway. He trails Tanya to the end of the hall and peers out a bubble-like Plexiglas window.

With a child's smile he says, "Reminds me of the gunner's spot in the Mitchell Bomber my granddad flew in during the Second World War." He takes a moment to check the grounds: burlap-covered perennials stretch above the snow, toward the swimming pool's chain-link fence a folded trampoline has its jumping bed and springs removed.

Tanya opens the door next to the Plexiglas structure and says, "This is where you will be bunking."

In the room their eyes lock; Gavin drops his bag and places his hands on Tanya's shoulders.

She slips her arms behind his back, locks her hands, and squeezes him saying, "I'm so happy you're here."

Gavin smothers her lips tenderly at first. Movement in his periphery makes him pause. He sees a grinning young lady, taller than Tanya but with the same dimpled cheeks.

Tanya twists her head and says, "Oh, this is my sister, Carolyn."

Carolyn extends her hand and gives Gavin a kiss on the cheek, then, while still holding his hand, she says, "So you're the mad trapper Tan's been talking about."

Gavin blushes. The shiver down his spine short-circuits his response.

"I've put the water on," Carolyn adds and leaves.

Tanya pecks Gavin's lips and they follow Carolyn.

At the alcove, Gavin notices a stack of telephone messages for Mr. Thoburn. In the living room he tries the leather-covered sofa and sits on its edge to accept a cup of tea. Shifting back, Gavin sinks more than expected and floods his saucer.

While Tanya places a paper napkin under Gavin's cup, Carolyn asks, "How's the snow north of Barrie?"

"Great, there were several skiing on Mount Saint Louis."

"Good, I have reservations in Collingwood for the weekend."

After Tanya pours Gavin another tea, Carolyn asks, "Tanya, mind if I use your ski boots, I can't find mine?"

Tanya frowns and says, "Sure, go ahead."

When Carolyn returns to the kitchen, Tanya says to Gavin, "With all the razzle-dazzle of Christmas I haven't done much training; how about going for a run before dinner?"

"Suits me, where'll we go?"

"High Park has little snow and next to no traffic."

Later in the afternoon and fifteen minutes into the run Tanya says, "I'm determined to make the Ontario Team for those Canada Games Scott talks about. The results he showed me aren't all that hot."

"Can you improve that much?"

"I did nine minutes 53 seconds in my first crack at 3,000-metres; if I trim 30 seconds I'd be in there. I sure won't if I don't try."

Gavin swallows hard, but suddenly remembers how miserable he felt when Pete ridiculed his hopes. He raises his arm, like a cavalry captain giving the signal to charge, and says, "Go for it!" Misery grips Gavin when he realizes how close he came to smothering her optimism.

In the crisp air, under the arched lights, to the rhythm of their footfalls, they pass darkened dressing rooms, snowed-over fields, and lovers maximizing the convenient parking.

On the drive back to Strathearn Boulevard, Gavin's head twists incessantly trying to absorb every aspect of the city.

Later at a high school reunion get-together, Tanya's friend inserts a video of their high school graduation party. During the diploma presentations of the video Gavin excuses himself to check the punch. When he returns, he stops abruptly at the sight of Tanya doing wide-open back somersaults above the trampoline with Thoburns' blue spruce wavering in the background.

Next evening, before leaving for the big dance, Gavin grimaces in the vestibule mirror. He feels like an imposter in a rented tuxedo. Moments later his chin drops when Tanya comes gliding down the stairs in her black jersey slit dress with emerald satin border. He senses he is playing a role in a debutante movie and smiles thinking not five months ago he pumped gas for a living.

Following two post-dance receptions they arrive home at 2:00 a.m. and change into casual attire. Downstairs, Tanya puts water to boil while Gavin moves through the alcove to the living room. He notices a doubling of Mr. Thoburn's messages on the credenza.

They sprawl on the living room rug amongst a nest of cushions and sip hot chocolate ignoring the barely audible movie channel. A telephone call disrupts Gavin's efforts at getting Tanya in a half nelson. Tanya gropes her way to the phone.

A female voice asks, "Is this the residence of Mr. Reginald Thoburn?"

"It is."

"This is Francine Brunet calling from Montreal, I'm one of your father's assistants. We were—working on a report in his room—when your father suddenly felt a tightness in his chest and pain under his left arm. I called the manager of the building. He summoned an ambulance."

"Just a moment please, I'll get my mother." Tanya sprints up the curved stairway unaware of her dishevelled state. She knocks and enters. Her mother is motionless.

"Mom, Mom," Tanya calls, but her mother doesn't respond. Tanya nudges her mother's leg.

Her mom's body springs from the eiderdown as though 220 volts had short-circuited her waterbed and demands, "What is it!"

"Dad's in the hospital! He became ill in his room, she—they—called the ambulance." Tanya reaches for the extension, but her mother has already clutched it.

"Hello, Mrs. Thoburn speaking."

"It's Francine Brunet. We were finishing our spring advertising report for Quebec when your husband had sudden chest pain and started gasping."

"Where did they take him?"

"Montreal General."

"Was he ... still conscious?"

"Barely."

"I see—thanks." Mrs. Thoburn drops the receiver and her eyes glaze while her jaw clenches highlighting every wrinkle she ever had. She relaxes somewhat and scans a bedside photograph. Her chin puckers as her stare settles on her climbing the waterfalls in Ocho Rios, Jamaica during her honeymoon.

Tanya hugs her mother and says, "We should check how he is."

When Mrs. Thoburn doesn't respond, Tanya creeps out of the room. Bracing her left hand on the banister, she bounds down the steps two-at-a-time and calls information.

"Yes, we have admitted a Mr. Thoburn. He's in intensive care in the cardiac unit."

"May I speak with the doctor involved?"

"No, but we should have a report within the hour." Tanya frowns, replaces the receiver slowly and returns to her mother.

Gavin nonchalantly jacks up the volume, tucks a cushion under his head, and watches Humphrey Bogart and Katharine Hepburn as they scramble through the rapids in the *African Queen*.

With Tanya's next call, she learns her dad is over the crisis, but it'll take time to assess the damage. When Tanya relays this information, her mother remains staring at the ceiling.

Next morning a solemn Mrs. Thoburn books the first flight to Montreal. Carolyn, figuring she can't alter her father's situation, continues her planned ski trip.

"Your father," Mrs. Thoburn reports later in the day to Tanya, "had a cardiac infarct. The extent of the damage is unknown. We talked for fifteen minutes. He's out of immediate danger."

"Oh, that's great!"

"Yes," Mrs. Thoburn replies with a soft, slow voice.

"And how are you mother?"

"I'm fine; why do you ask?"

"Oh, nothing."

"I'll call after my next visit—has Carolyn gone?"

"Yes, said she'd keep in touch."

"Please see Jenny gets the Christmas wrappings out for pickup Wednesday. I want the place in order for my Eastern Star meeting Thursday. Take care."

"All right Mother."

Tanya returns to the living room looking more relaxed and inserts the first tape she sees. It's Neil Diamond's, "Love on the Rocks."

Chapter 9

In Windsor, Scott Cassidy rushes a couple of steps to evade a swerving van angling into the parking lot of a Brewer's Retail. A block later on Wyandotte Street he enters the Captain's Table Tavern. It is dimly lit and heavy with cigarette smoke.

Rawlins Martin, Scott's high school teammate, sits in a booth under a mock porthole. Rawlins beams from beneath a shock of black hair. When he spots Scott, he stands and unfolds his eighty-eight kilogram mass.

They exchange congratulatory slaps on each other's backs reminiscent of when they were '79 Windsor High School Football Champions. "How are you enjoying school in the boondocks?" Rawlins says.

Scott delays his response when he catches sight of the approaching waitress' open denim jacket. It is the only garment she wears above her waist. "Nice set of lungs," Scott mumbles. When the waitress arrives, Scott points to what Rawlins was drinking. He then answers Rawlins' earlier question, "No complaints about the boonies ... made a good start ... hit just under 14 metres with the sixteen. I didn't win the Ontario Outdoors but I'll get those bastards indoors." Scott purses his lips and slowly nods his head affirmatively.

"Do ya miss football?"

"A bit, but I don't miss a coach like Grasschuck who never took time to figure the real reason our team won. In track you do things on your own; there's no guessing what an individual contributes, performance says it all."

"What are ya aiming for?" Rawlins asks, his eyes riveted on Scott.

"To make the Ontario Team for the Canada Games in Thunder Bay this summer." Scott pauses to appreciate the feminine pulchritude of the waitress while she unloads his mug; "Perhaps the Commonwealth Games the following year, go that route."

"What're you doing with the weights?"

"Basic lifts."

"What're you using?"

"What do you mean?" Scott replies raising his heavy blond eyebrows.

"R-O-I-D-S," Rawlins spells out.

"Hell no! I wouldn't mess with them. All those stories going 'round, that's not for me."

"Don't be a child, those fears are all a pile of crap. Guys on the football team have been using them for years; most of the throwers in Nevada are on them; otherwise they couldn't be competitive."

"Have you actually seen anyone take them?"

"I'm on them myself! Couldn't keep a position on the football team if I didn't. Of course, I follow directions closely from the boys downtown at the lifting club."

Rawlins takes a healthy swig from his stein, leans closer to Scott and confides, "I can handle 335 in the clean and 425 for the squat. That's a helluva change let me tell ya. No side effects, except I'm more horny, but who minds that?" A self-satisfied smile creeps over Rawlins' face.

Scott lowers his head in an audible sigh. Then with half his teeth exposed in a twisted mouth, he leans forward with his glassy stare levelled at Fred Rawlins. Scott's lips start twitching as if he was trying to say something. He exhales slowly, turns his head away from Rawlins and is speechless. He readjusts his buttocks to the chair's back and assesses the magnitude of Rawlins Martin's improvement. Incredible! How could this unimpressive high school footballer have been able to achieve that? Scott wonders whether he should have ignored his father's contempt for everything American and gone Stateside to university.

Rawlins suppresses a grin. This is the first time the almighty Scott has taken him seriously.

A pensive Scott remembers how Rawlins xeroxed his best clippings into a resume that he circulated to forty smaller American universities. Three months later he accepted a half scholarship at Central Nevada. Gall and drug-assisted strength building launched Rawlins into the big leagues—Shit!

They leave an hour later to check the holiday basketball tournament at their old high school. At half time of the final game, they meet tall Sally from Queens at the refreshment booth.

Scott, so possessed with the idea of steroids, is oblivious to Sally's coolness to him.

Rawlins suggests they finish the evening at Don Cherry's Bar. Scott excuses himself.

At home he finds his father sprawled in a reclining chair reading; his gangly mother divides her attention between her ironing and the television set.

"Join me with a brew Son?"

"Sure."

Mr. Cassidy opens another lager for Scott and points to an easy chair next to him. They chat a few minutes about Scott's visit with his uncle on the Sudbury Police Force. It was this uncle who convinced Scott to go to Laurentian.

Mr. Cassiday after a pause, says, "You know Son, much of athletic achievement is in your attitude. If an athlete convinces himself he is better than his competitors he will overpower them. With a name in sports you're set for life."

Scott doesn't respond. When the sports cast is over, they have their usual game of rummy five hundred at a cent a point. Scott collects a dollar ten from his dad and they prepare the foldaway bed in the living room. In stashing the magazine rack with newspapers, Scott smiles at a library book entitled, *Psyching Yourself to Victory in Sport.*

His dad pours himself a glass of milk to comfort his burning stomach. But before going upstairs Scott's dad returns to the living room and asks, "Are you comfortable enough?"

"Not too bad Dad."

"Had you thought about my suggestions on mental preparation? What wouldn't I give to be your age again and know what I know now!"

"I'll try using it, Dad."

"Don't try, dammit just do it."

Scott cringes at the full wrath of Captain Cassidy of the Windsor Police Force who is almost two metres tall.

Then relaxing the knot in his brow, Captain Cassidy says softly, "Boy Scouts are the only ones rewarded for trying in this world."

"Good night Dad," Scott says with an unruffled voice and turns off the table lamp. But anger bursts inside him. He hates his makeshift sleeping arrangement: the ridge of the discontinuous mattress crimps his thigh. His bed is dismantled in the garage, while his younger brother's drums fill his old bedroom. The streetlight beams into a corner of the living room striking a calendar portrait of Queen Elizabeth II. Scott senses the eyes of royalty are scrutinizing his life and he is not measuring up. When he was a kid, Queen Elizabeth's picture hung beside the piano. In those days, he couldn't stop practising; he loved taking lessons from his aunt. He figures the Queen was proud of him then. One summer when he was at music camp in Michigan, his dad moved the piano into the new recreation room in the basement. The piano never sounded right since.

But Scott's biggest concern is coming to grips with steroids. He mulls over everything he has heard or read. In the morning he decides to stay clean. However, before returning to Sudbury, he spends another evening at the Captain's Table Tavern squeezing Rawlins for more details on what he is doing.

Chapter 10

Back on Strathearn Boulevard a chime dings at the front door. Tanya says to Gavin, "I wonder who that could be?" When four more follow in rapid succession, she says, "Who the hell's that!" She stomps to the door clearing a stray strand from her forehead.

"Ah Aunt Mildred, come in."

Mildred coughs twice and signals the cab driver to fetch her two bags. With arms folded and chin raised she says, "I do wish Constance would telephone when she can't meet me; I felt silly waiting and looking for an hour. Well, never mind, I made it in spite of that driver who doesn't understands English."

"Yes, we're sorry Aunt Mildred but—"

"Constance still in bed is she?"

"No, you haven't heard—"

"Heard what!"

"Father's had a heart attack. Mother's with him in Montreal; he seems to be over the greatest danger."

"Oh! I'm sorry—how is Constance managing?"

"She's devastated."

"Poor dear, she's been so supportive all these years, to have something like this happen when things were getting comfortable—must be distressing." Mildred interrupts her reaction a moment to hand the driver a twenty. Then continues, "Where's Carolyn?"

"Skiing."

"You mean you're alone?"

"Not exactly. My friend, Gavin, from the university is visiting for a few days."

"He's here with you alone? Now Tanya!" Aunt Mildred coughs and shuffles her feet.

"Mother has arranged your favourite room looking out on the blue spruce. Let me get your luggage."

Before Mildred answers Gavin appears and says, "Hi."

"Aunt Mildred, this is Gavin." Turning to Gavin, Tanya mentions, "Aunt Mildred's from Ottawa."

Aunt Mildred nods curtly and redirects her attention to Tanya.

Gavin says, "I'll get d' bags." When Aunt Mildred doesn't object, Gavin grasps a valise handle in each hand.

Aunt Mildred wrinkles her forehead, and with her hand concealing her mouth and Gavin half way up the stairs, says, "French?"

The pupils of Tanya's eyes enlarge and her stomach shrivels; she gazes at her slippers and exhales slowly. Tanya closes her eyes thinking, this couldn't be the same aunt that brought me to Europe on two happy occasions.

Tanya's gaze drifts to the ceiling.

Mildred tucks her purse under her arm, straightens her shoulders, and climbs the curved stairway with deliberate steps. Before unpacking, Mildred calls her cousin. Two hours later, she returns downstairs, puts on her coat, and when her taxi arrives, says, "I'm leaving for a musical presentation at Roy Thomson Hall."

Next morning Aunt Mildred joins Tanya and Gavin for a silent breakfast. When her cab stops, Aunt Mildred says to Tanya, "Goodbye dear, I'm sorry about having to rush off to see Constance."

As the taxi swerves, Tanya twists her head from side to side remembering Mildred's favourite expression to her mother, "Oh how travel broadens one's perspective on people."

That evening Tanya suggests they attend another house party with some of her school friends. "It's at a heritage home: high ceilings, brass claw-footed bathtubs, and bidets."

Gavin wonders what a bidet is but doesn't ask. He ponders how many other things he will be ignorant of before the evening is over.

They arrive late. After he has fielded several questions about the dry cold in Sudbury, a young lady asks Gavin in French, "Whatever happened to the Dionne Quintuplets?"

While Gavin replies in French, Tanya takes the opportunity to drift to the punch bowl.

A red-faced gentleman in a navy blue blazer, precisely-parted blond hair, and a finely trimmed mustache, leans toward Tanya and says, "Sorry about Reg. My dad and I sailed with him some years ago at the Boulevard Club. I'm Fred Langdon," He extends his hand.

"Hi, I'm Tanya."

"Yes, I remember you from my graduating year at Forest Hill. You were on the swim team and ran on the school four x 400 metre relay."

"Yes," Tanya replies smiling.

"Do you still compete?"

"I'll be trying for the Ontario Team for the Canada Games as a runner."

"Really, I'm expecting—I should say hoping—to make it in the laser class in sailing."

"Well, good luck to you," Tanya replies and turns cautiously holding her full glass away from her rib-knit sweater. Walking away she asks herself what's up with this debonair young man. Then she settles it thinking he must be from Royal Military College or an acting troupe presenting, *The Charge of the Light Brigade.*

"And to you too," Fred replies lifting his glass in a mock toast to Tanya's back.

Tanya observes that Gavin has shifted to another gathering. She sips her fruit punch and reflects on how their groups' parties are losing momentum. And yet again it's probably me, she chuckles to herself.

When Gavin suppresses his second yawn chatting with two Havergal College girls, Tanya joins him and whispers, "About ready to go?"

"Sure."

As she drives, Tanya glances at a limp Gavin beside her and asks, "What's up?"

"Well, I've had it with the hockey talk of the lousy Leafs, the advantages of the 305 Ferrari over the Porsche 944, and the best things to do during a Bermuda holiday." He didn't add that he felt he was wasting his time and that he could be training harder in Sudbury.

But he immediately regrets making these comments for Tanya's face sags and headlight beams from oncoming traffic reflect tears seeping down her cheeks.

On New Year's Eve, Tanya opens a bottle of Bordeaux to accompany the ordered pizza. But neither the wine nor the video *Quiet Cool*, alter her owlish face.

Chapter 11

Dirty falling snow at Barrie changes to a fluffy white by the time the Greyhound passengers plod into the Parry Sound restaurant. At Sudbury's Four Corners, Gavin flags a cab. In the back seat with arms interlaced Gavin and Tanya exchange smiles but not words. Tanya, for the first time, ponders the smoothness of her cruise through life in the fast lane.

The taxi driver whistles an accompaniment to a Billy Joel tune as he drives down Paris Street. He takes furtive glances in his rear view mirror at his pensive passengers. Only the odd snowflake hangs in the air when Gavin unfolds his wallet.

They change into running attire and soon are striding down snow-covered South Bay Road. To the left, they pass columns of smoke drifting above the chimneys. On the right, slices of snow cling precipitously to birch twigs. Down the road, on both sides, clumps of snow smother the conifer boughs. At the five-kilometre point Tanya turns back. Gavin runs four kilometers further to Moonlight Beach, circles the parking lot and retraces his tracks. Back on the main road, he keeps on the left-hand shoulder facing the traffic. As he approaches the university, a gust from the north smarts his earlobes; he unrolls his toque further.

The following day the Laurentian distance runners meet for an orientation session on outdoor training with their coach. Seven athletes huddle on the stairs of the Ben Avery Building overlooking the sports fields. Dressed for outside, they listen to the coach: "This will be our only outside practice as a group; Tanya and Lisa, I suggest you turn at the top of Cardiac Hill; the rest can follow through as far as you wish on the Moonlight Beach trail; if you haven't kept up your running I suggest you don't overdo it and turn back when your coordination falters. Fresh snow makes it slow, some of you will have more trouble than others coping with it." Tanner coughs a couple of times, searches for an elusive tissue, and adds, "Remember, these runs consolidate an endurance base for the faster stuff indoors. The more you get in without severely draining yourselves, the better. Spread your hard efforts over reasonable time periods."

During Tanner's talk, Tanya's attention drifts to the repetitious, muffled, scratchy sounds outside. Shifting her gaze to the sports field, she notices a solitary skier silhouetted against the white snow. A mask of hoarfrost covers his eyebrows and mustache. The skier's disdain for his encrusted face and his pugnacious double poling into the wind kindles a spark of delight in her. When Tanya's attention returns to her coach, she hears him dispelling a freshman's anxiety about freezing his lungs. As he descends the front steps, the encroaching five o'clock darkness makes Gavin pout. But he remembers the winter solstice has passed and that each clear day will bring five more minutes of the sun's presence. The sharp northeast wind bites his cheeks as he heads down Voyageur Boulevard. He notes, with envy, Tanya unroll her toque to cover her face. Gavin regrets not having allowed his favorite head cover to dry adequately after yesterday's workout. He removes his gloves to unzip the concealed hood in his jacket's collar, but the group at South Bay Road turn right and out of the wind. Gavin decides he can get by without his hood.

Running next to Andy Tanner, Gavin asks, "Will that raw feeling I get in my throat when I run outdoors stay with me all winter?"

"Not if you control the pace. Cut the quality in the bitter cold; extend the quantity."

As they run, the road swerves between two mountains and so offers protection from the gusts of wind. A bright moon stalks them through the scraggly tree line. The crunch from each footfall sinks in pitch when they shift from asphalt to gravel. At the top of Cardiac Hill, Tanya and Lisa turn back.

The others continue over a well-packed skidoo trail to Moonlight Beach. On the return, Gavin excuses himself from the group to explore a snowmobile path to Perch Lake. His shadow dims as he drifts deeper into the umbrella of birch and aspen. A snowshoe hare bounds up a snow bank, stares at the intruder, and plunges for cover in the thickets. Gavin perceives his body is like that of the hare's, constructed to endure with the environment in a violent yet harmonious way. He remembers from class how the wild hare's heart rate has ten fewer beats per minute than the domesticated rabbit's when moving the same blood at rest. The professor claimed the wild hare's stronger heart ejected more blood per beat.

With primeval pleasure, Gavin skims up and down inclines and around bends in the frosty air. He smiles thinking this must be what Arvo calls "man's natural state." He senses a kinship with his ancestors who settled this country as well as with the thriving animals. The trail changes into a wider abandoned mining road. He brushes hoar frost from his eyebrows as he approaches the lake. Along the crusted shore, each shoe strike gives a wafer biscuit, biting sensation.

Some time later he reenters the sports building and notes he has been gone for one hour and thirty-two minutes. He crawls out of his limp garments and shakes off the remaining ice crystals. In the shower, he inhales deeply and starts singing *Chevalier de la table ronde*. Thoughts of Tanya's father make him wonder if more regular physical activity could have neutralized his problem.

That evening, puzzled about Mr. Thoburn's lifestyle and his recent cardiac infarct, Gavin abandons his study of cell membrane dynamics to share his thinking with Tanya.

"I wondered about the same thing," Tanya says after listening to Gavin. She adds, "He's always thrown himself totally into advertising. Salvaging projects others had fumbled has been his specialty."

Gavin asks, "How much physical activity did he do?"

"He did a lot of tennis, golfed, and sailed but more recently, photography was his chief hobby. Even that he set aside lately."

Seven hundred kilometres east of Sudbury, Reginald Thoburn frowns at the wires attached to him. He probes under his ill-fitting gown and squeezes skin at an electrode. He is curious as to the effect it might have on his monitor. But before he looks up something more striking happens. He realizes the extent of floating mass at his midriff. At that moment he resolves to change his priorities and never again neglect what his Sunday School Teacher called the temple of his soul. Then he reflects on how easily he drifted into careless living. On three successive vacations he had quit smoking, only to start on a pipe and then on cigarettes as deadlines challenged. Head office's reassurance of hiring sufficient competent assistants for him never materialized. He never complained; he actually enjoyed outmanoeuvreing his opposition and earning bonuses—the fewer involved the greater the reward. He smiles thinking how his recent Labatt's "new product design" booted him into a feature in the *Globe and Mail's* Business Section.

Remembering how many things in life he has left undone makes him cringe. Has he another chance? The cynical retirement speech of James Grant, his predecessor stepping down as Head of Eastern Operations, has always bothered him. Grant's only son was hooked on crack before he left high school. Thoburn now reflects on how his promotion cost him his weekends with Tanya and her swimming world. Tanya, he feels, will make it. His eldest daughter Carolyn, he wasn't so sure.

A dear but a parasite, he mumbles to himself when he thinks of Carolyn. By the time he realized this, correction time was long past. Carolyn was too busy living to share family chores or pursue a career path with any gusto. Life, she believed, was a constant blast. He considers his marriage of twenty-five years. There have been many highs and some lows but recently his missing of dinners with his wife and Carolyn had become the rule rather than the exception. Constance as a result has carved her own path in the social world and most of it does not include him. Her knack for entertaining had been a particular asset in the early years. Guests flocked with their families for special occasions.

She provided mechanical toys for the toddlers, board games for the youngsters, and a sound-proof recreational room for the teenagers. The screened-off swimming pool had an abundance of heated Walt Disney caricatured towels. Her gastronomical delights for adults ranged from cheesy broccoli linguini to exotic dishes of squid and rabbit.

Constance seemed happy doing volunteer Red Cross and Eastern Star work. Yet, he had to admit, the air fuelling the flame of their affection lacked oxygen.

On returning to Toronto, three weeks later, Thoburn starts overhauling his life. He discards the carefully saved messages. His accountant confronts him with the necessity of dissolving the mortgage on his residence if he wishes to retire.

A month later Mr. Thoburn's physician refers him to Dr. Terence Kavanagh, a leader in guiding heart patients in physical activity rehabilitation. When a treadmill stress test at 75 percent of Thoburn's predicted ability to suck in oxygen is pain free, Thoburn commences more serious physical exercise. His walking is monitored once a week on the Toronto Rehabilitation track. After which, he joins the group discussions. Kavanagh states that many patients can restyle their lives and keep their jobs. Thoburn senses he can't control his commitment in the advertising business, which for him was all or nothing.

During a dinner, Thoburn decides to share his intentions with his wife. He pauses while sipping a ginger ale to say, "Constance, we could make a chateau out of the cottage by putting in a concrete foundation and totally remodeling the rooms. There's nothing to burying the water line. With eleven permanent homes on the lake we wouldn't be isolated."

"And leave my friends in the city, no chance!"

"We could maintain an apartment in the city as well."

"And live like paupers?"

"No."

"I can't see it!" Constance says, folds her arms, stands, and leaves the table.

Chapter 12

Yes, Tanya, I'm leaving your father—it's been a good twenty-five years—but we're charting different courses. I think he's giving up on life. Imagine living in a cottage—selling our home. Can you conceive forsaking everything after we've made so many improvements?"

"But Mom—," Tanya said, standing up and squeezing the receiver as if trying to strangle her mother's words.

"Yes, dear, I know it'll be difficult but you're grown up, you have interests outside the family." Mrs. Thoburn paused then said, "Tanya, I tell you, there's more to life than living with a recluse who wants to spend his remaining days snapping photographs. I can't do it Tanya."

"But Mom, he needs you more than ever."

"Well, he'd better ask Francine Brunet to look after him. I still have years ahead of me and I'm not going out to pasture with him. Good night Tanya, I do hope you understand. I'm sorry to trouble you but I think I've … we've provided for you remarkably well. When circumstances change we all must react."

"Yes, Mother, good night." Tanya replies, choking on her words.

That night Tanya has disruptive spurts of adrenalin coursing through her blood. Her mind the next day never ceases to buzz.

She attends practice hoping to block her brain's automatic replay. But in recovery jogs, the dilemma restarts. Gone, she knows, are family weekends at the cottage: her father galloping on the beach tussling his daughters for a soccer ball; the pots they crafted from the creek's blue clay and dried in the summer sun; her mother squatting on a Hudson's Bay blanket knitting beneath the pine boughs as CBC Radio cracked the spring air.

In Tanya's next repeat of three laps, she runs fast and forgets her troubles— until the next rest interval. Her thoughts then plummet to the evening when she informed her mother of her dad's illness. Her mother's devastated look still torments her. It's true, Tanya recalls, her father did discuss changes in his life during a telephone conversation; she remembers agreeing; however, she didn't conceive the change including her home and her mother. Tanya's despair, like a gyroscopic mass, can't be shaken off. Her misery sinks deeper when she remembers how little in common she has with her high school friends. Although she considers Gavin exciting, she needs more. But she doesn't know what that is.

The coach nods for Tanya to start her next run. There is no shortage of electricity coursing through her discordant body.

"Good work Tanya, that's great running. Take three minutes before your last repeat."

Tanya glints with pleasure. No matter what, she promises herself, she will keep running during this hell; when she runs, she feels in control.

But thoughts of her father soon bewilder her again. She knows her father's tenacity at seeing projects through made him the backbone of the firm. Quitting, when his doctor hadn't ordered it, wasn't his style. Yet, she recalls him dejectedly stating when she picked him up at the airport one weekend, "Isn't there more to life than trying to get people to tank up on Texaco?"

When Tanya returns to residence, she plods up the stairs. Her suppressed tears are ready to explode. Home without her parents' constant banter is impossible to imagine. It wasn't as though they fought or were nasty with each other.

She enters her apartment. When she hears the girls flitting about over a cake for Janet's birthday, she drops her sports bag and decides to see Gavin. She ambles down the stairs and knocks on the open door.

Gavin in sweats is perched on an easy chair and alone. He drops the article he has been reading and watches as she drags herself in; her normally precise blond hair has nests of frizzy strands, her sweat top collar has a reverse fold.

Seeing her puffy eyes, he approaches and softly says, "Is it your father?"

"Yes and no. He's healthy enough, but he's decided to retire and live in a remodeled cottage. Mother won't go. They're splitting."

Gavin notices Tanya's cheeks twitch as she fights back tears. "Not much you can do Tanya, let them sort it out."

Tanya's head darts up in a frown.

Gavin continues, "It takes getting used to, but in some ways a person ends up stronger. I had to look after myself in a hurry." Gavin's voice tails off; for in spite of what he says, thinking about the family support he might have had, makes him nostalgic.

Tanya maintains her tensed cheeks and clenched jaw for a few more seconds. Finally she relaxes with a sigh and says, "I guess you're right." She removes her jacket.

Gavin places his hands on her shoulders, and he looks into her bewildered eyes and asks, "Has Tanner talked to you about special preparation for the Canada Games trials?"

"No."

"Well, it'll keep us humming when school's over. He wants the three of us in Sudbury. We have a couple of months training and if we make the Ontario Team, the actual Games in Thunder Bay."

But Tanya wasn't interested in her athletic future; she was suppressing another anxiety storm. When her forehead contorts, Gavin regrets what he has said and hugs her. She squeezes back fiercely then goes limp.

"I'm okay," she says and straightens her shoulders. "Better get back to Janet's party." She stares into Gavin's aquamarine eyes and her lips crinkle mirthfully while she stretches into the sleeves of her jacket

But the smile dissolves when she leaves. Breakups happen to others, not the model family she belongs to.

Chapter 13

Five months later, Tanya, Gavin, and Scott buckle up for the DC 10 flight to Thunder Bay and the Canada Games. At cruising altitude Scott, sitting next to the window, lowers his seat and jams a pillow against the side of the plane.

Gavin fumbles for the reclining device and suppresses a congratulatory grin as he stretches back thinking of Pete who told him he didn't have enough speed to be a runner. When he twists, his piece of shrapnel dangling from his neck rubs against his chest. He regrets not being able to share this moment with his father and grandfather.

Gavin glances at Tanya. He wasn't sure whether it was her heavy training, her nervousness over the coming Games, or her parents split, but she has been waspish the past three weeks. Today is an exception. When he sees her turn the *En Route* magazine to a description of the aircraft, he returns to the vertical. In a few moments, he says, "Must be something flying a craft like this. I wouldn't want to guess the number of gadgets it must have."

The next time Tanya sees the bored-looking stewardess she asks, "Would it be possible to visit the flight deck?"

"Let me clear it with the captain." The attendant's eyes liven and she disappears behind the restraining curtain. She returns in thirty seconds smiling. "Sure go ahead."

The stewardess's change intrigues Gavin. Had this special request added something different to her day? They glance at Scott propped against the window cuddling a pillow with his eyes closed and leave him.

A light-headed Gavin in the cockpit wonders whether all the windows weaken the structure. The complexity of the instrument panel has him shaking his head. Straightening from a leaning position, he says, "Nothing like my dad's 172 Cessna."

Tanya, bent over the console, mechanically tucks an obstructing lock out of her line of vision and peers from one gauge to another. With enlarged eyes she says, "Wouldn't I love a job like this?"

On that remark, Gavin notices the silver-haired captain's smile become a pensive squint. Does the captain question why so few females become commercial pilots? The power and the mystery of navigation through cirrus clouds at 7,000 metres gives Gavin the perception of the Greek God Zeus surveying his ethereal realm.

Approaching Thunder Bay, Tanya stretches her neck similar to a mother duck checking her brood. She follows the plane's descent over the coastal promontories of igneous rock. In sight of Thunder Bay, she taps Gavin's shoulder and nudges Scott. Pointing out the window she says, "There's the Sleeping Giant."

Before Gavin figures out what Tanya means, Scott, with barely parted eyelids, replies, "Big deal," and adds in a monotone, "don't get excited over a few rock ridges in water."

Gavin then remembers hearing of this phenomenon. He notices Tanya's chin sag as her pointing hand goes limp. She then clenches her teeth and glares intently at the seat in front of her.

As the plane banked for a landing, the roar of the jets turns to a scream as they intercept a crosswind. Gavin feels Zeus is getting even with them for Scott's rebuff.

With a few bounces, like an alpine skier hitting moguls, the pilot maneuvers in front of the terminal. When the pilot cuts the engines, Tanya reaches for her jacket in the overhead bin. Gavin observes her pause, smile, and gesture with an opening and closing of her hand at someone several seats back.

At the baggage retrieval area, a team member with neatly combed blond hair and a pencil line mustache chats with Tanya.

"Gavin, this is Frederic Langdon, he was at a Christmas party we attended in Toronto. He's on the Sailing Team."

"How you doing?" Gavin asks extending his hand.

"Jim-dandy," Frederic replies, clutching Gavin's hand enthusiastically.

What's up with this joker, Gavin wonders? He then fills the prolonged silence with, "Good, good, glad to meet you," and retreats toward the conveyor belt. Gavin grips his bags and follows Scott, who has his luggage and is now inquiring about transportation to the Athletes' Village.

Tanya finishes explaining the day and time of her final event to Frederic. When she retrieves her bags and moves to join Scott and Gavin, Frederic says, "I'm taking a cab to ensure my laser tackle doesn't get damaged with my luggage; would you care to join?"

"Sure, sure!" Tanya replies. But when she turns to invite Gavin and Scott she sees them at the baggage room exit.

"Dammit!" Tanya snarls. She drops her bags to chase.

Frederic clutches her arm and says, "Don't worry, we'll catch them at residence."

Tanya shakes Frederic's squeeze and darts closer until she sees Gavin and Scott have already tossed their bags in the luggage van. She slowly returns to Frederic.

On the athletes' bus, Gavin slinks to a seat close to the silent Scott. When he notices Tanya and Frederic zip by in a cab his lips form a spastic smile.

The athletes' bus takes an extra thirty minutes as two athletes file claims for lost luggage. While they wait, Scott repeats in a barely audible voice, "I'll pulverize those hacks next Thursday."

On arrival there is no sign of Tanya. Gavin figures Tanya's withdrawal could be her way of avoiding further confrontations with Scott. Gavin decides to look for her at the next meal. He arrives early. When he is almost finished his roast beef, he notices Tanya enter with her sailing friend. Gavin debates whether to join. By the time he overcomes his bruised pride, the vacant seats beside Tanya are filled.

Gavin trains the next day on the grass fields near Confederation College Residence. He follows Tanner's schedule precisely; he regrets Tanner's wife is expecting and so Tanner could not join them. Gavin didn't see, nor does he bother to seek, Tanya that day.

Two days later he takes the shuttle to the track stadium. When he tries to enter the nearest gate for the shortest route an official points to the opposite entrance and says, "Athletes enter by the south gate and please show your identification."

The stadium is buzzing when Gavin enters. A starter fires the pistol for the electrical timing operators at the finish line; the group surrounding the pole vault make certain the uprights can be shifted freely toward the take off or toward the landing area. Three ladies with clip boards take notes on the different colours of the relay exchange lines. Gavin watches athletes with fleur-de-lis sweats scoot around the track with a vengeance. In the lower seats at the media's urging, visiting VIPS babble into cattail-shaped microphones.

Gavin floats through his prescribed workout. When he sees how strenuously other athletes train, he fears Tanner has given him too little work. This leaves him charged with energy, almost restless.

When Gavin notices Tanya jogging easily on the outside lane, he crosses over and asks, "Could I talk with you a moment?" His eyes search hers.

Tanya stops jogging and says, "Where have you been? I've looked and waited for you all over the place, now I'm fed up—completely." She resumes her run.

"But—Oh forget it," Gavin says, and returns to where he left his unattended kit bag.

On the Thursday before the Sunday qualifying round, Gavin has another session at the stadium; he wants to try his new spikes over the actual water jump barrier. After the workout he ties his new, wet spikes on the handle of his shoulder bag and leaves his bag with others from Ontario while he goes to the washroom. When he returns, he can't find his spikes.

He scans the hundreds of athletes for the distinct yellow and black colour of his shoes. Then he climbs the stadium stairs for a better view. There is no sign of his shoes. Gradually athletes and coaches drift to waiting buses.

Gavin shakes his head in disbelief and with a feeble motion slings his bag strap over his shoulder. He makes a final tour of the track, thinking someone may have tried them, and found they didn't fit. He presses his lips together thinking how ineffective his worn-down training spikes would be on the wet barrier. After a futile lap of searching, he decides to cover the fields outside the stadium. He returns crestfallen and sees neither an athlete nor a shuttle bus. He yanks his white Canada Games cap over his eyes, folds his arms, and collapses with a moan on a bleacher seat.

A young lady, leaving the press booth at the top of the stadium, notices him. As she passes Gavin in descending the stairs, she asks, "Are you abandoned?"

Gavin lifts his cap, blinks a couple of times to confirm the dainty *retroussé* nose of the person posing the question, and replies, "Cynthia, isn't it?"

"Why yes, and you're?"

"Gavin."

"Of course," she says with a generous smile and extends her hand.

Gavin grasps her hand and says, "I missed the last bus looking for my lost spikes."

"Those you race with?"

"Yeah," Gavin says dryly.

"I'm going back to residence after a stop at the pool if it's a help."

"Sure thing." He picks up his kit and joins her brisk walk. As they leave the stadium, Gavin reflects on the lively time he had with her in Kingston, before Scott's antics. Connecting with an amiable brunet in snug Levis was hardly what he expected after losing his spikes.

"Here," she calls and points to a Tilden van with the letters C.A.S.A. emblazoned on a white piece of cardboard taped to the driver's door.

"I've a few forms to drop off for the swim meet tomorrow," she says as she engages the reverse and creeps backwards.

"What's your official function?"

"I'm doing my placement with C.A.S.A." When Gavin wrinkles his brow, she adds, "In my Business Administration

Master's Program I chose to do practical work with a Sports Governing Body. I'm involved with the Canadian Amateur Swimming Association."

While parking at the pool, she asks, "Why don't you come along?"

They enter the side door, show their identification to a bored security officer, and enter the unlit pool. They angle toward the awards dais.

Gavin observes the new building's smell of paint obliterates most of the chlorine odour. He pauses by the victory stand when Cynthia mounts the steps to the announcer's booth. In the sparse illumination from the underwater lights, he watches the green waves slap the side gutters with heartbeat regularity. The moving waters' muffled echo bounces from the ceiling. Gavin feels immersed in a giant cavern.

Cynthia, not finding the person she is seeking, places a note on the announcer's table with a packet of papers.

"Let's leave by the front," Cynthia suggests, while pointing at a doorway next to a giant portrait of Queen Elizabeth II.

In the main lobby the flags of the provinces and territories undulate from the rafters sending a shiver of pride through Gavin. With people scattered over a vast land, Canadians are having an elite family reunion, and he is part of it.

While Gavin gazes, Cynthia sidles up and says, "By the way, I have an extra ticket for a reception at the Sheraton tonight; would you care to accompany me?"

Gavin lowers his head, turns to Cynthia, and says, "Sure."

"Pick you up at eight?"

"Fine."

At eight-fifteen Cynthia, in a white chiffon dress, and Gavin, in his red Ontario Team jacket and trousers, climb the stairs to the mezzanine floor at the Sheraton. A heavy tinkling of glass and excited chatter pervade the ballroom when they enter. Four bars, one at each corner, accommodate the thirsty. The hungry hover at rectangular tables' enticing trays: caviar, creamed meats, fish masked with aspic, and assorted sandwiches. A central circular table has a large cake, in Canada's geographical shape, with *Jeux Canada Games* written in green icing across its white top.

Outbursts of laughter erupt regularly as sporting moguls begin to relax after three successful days of Games' action. Cynthia exchanges business with the gentleman she missed at the pool and then makes a claim on the cake. Gavin, after taking advantage of his second gratuitous refreshment ticket, trades his five Ontario pins to representatives from the Yukon. While exchanging, he asks about Stewart Crossing Outfitters. He is disappointed no one from Whitehorse knows anything about it as that is where his mother works.

When shrimp no longer adorn the ice sculpture and sandwich trays appear ravished by ravens, Cynthia nudges her beaming face close to Gavin's and asks, "Would you care to catch the highlights of today's activities on TV in my room?"

Gavin smiles, rotates his palms up, and shrugs his shoulders in a why-not attitude.

They take the elevator to the twelfth floor. Seeing a sliding balcony door facing the bay, Gavin motions with his head for Cynthia to join him. They step into the moonlight. On the bay, strings of lights outline the watercraft drifting over the calm waters. Above the bay, crimson streaks bid farewell to another majestic day.

When Cynthia curls closer to Gavin's shoulder, he drapes his arm on the nape of her neck, smiles into her amber eyes, and feels his lumbering heart soar into overdrive. A fresh breeze rustles her hair, and her crystal earrings sparkle in the moonlight. Their lips meet gently.

Some time later Gavin whispers, "I think I'd better be getting back, it's past the midnight curfew."

"No problem, I have to deliver lane assignments to the swim coaches' mail boxes in residence for tomorrow."

They readjust their attire and descend to the lobby. Cynthia gathers the forms from the Games office and drives to residence. Before walking through Village security, she hands Gavin half the pile.

"Some people's work never ends, eh!" A plump guard mentions while nodding his head.

"I guess not," Cynthia replies, resisting a smile.

Chapter 14

Wonder what's up? Gavin ponders when three calls to Cynthia bring no response. Puzzling over tactics obliterates romantic thoughts as race day approaches.

Gavin chooses the grass fields outside the stadium for his 3,000-metre steeplechase warmup. When his event is called, he reports to the Athletes' Control Centre. After clearance, he reclines on one of the many tumbling mats and uses his kit bag as a pillow. Gavin visualizes the most famous entry he has made in his training journal: circled in red is August 12, 1981, 3:55 p.m. He sees 3:35 on the stadium clock. From his cordoned area beside the track, he scans the crowd witnessing this fourth day of track and field. His right hand drops to his side pocket zipper. He lifts and lowers his zipper tab as he considers what it is about sport that has fostered these Games? Three days ago at old Fort William, he relished the stories of sinewy fur traders reveling in ad-lib athletic contests at their yearly gatherings. Did the Canada Games reflect the human need to exhibit and celebrate physical prowess?

The zipper jams. He glances to see 3:40 on the stadium clock. Mindful of Tanner's advice, "Keep active once you finish your main warmup," he stands and runs on the spot.

A sudden roar from the crowd raises goose pimples down Gavin's back. A whiff of smoke from the concessions conjures up memories of frying walleyes on campfires and he wishes he had never heard of track and field. No—he figures competition provides the goal that gives his life meaning. Grinding his molars, he resolves to defy that part of him that shouts, ease up, when his legs and lungs crave respite.

A gust of wind hits his face. He raises his gaze above the grandstand where massive, puffball-like clouds streak across the sky as though chased by some all-powerful deity. He marvels at nature's abundance of energy and wishes he could transmute more into his limbs.

He coughs three times into the sleeve of his sweatsuit trying to clear a parched throat. Gavin needs to urinate, but he can't leave. He shakes each leg twice to insure the earlier numbness has gone. Again he curses his stupidity for getting sucked into a sport that causes his body to float like a helium balloon and his mind to somersault in multiaxial directions.

However … this isn't any race; it's the Canada Games and it reaches the living rooms of the nation. He yawns, and when he realizes from his psychology course that it's a sign of nervousness, he tries to hide his action. His hoarse throat makes him regret not having packed a water bottle.

He reclines again on the tumbling mats. With his head buried in his arms, he's rehearsing each phase of his race when a hand settles on his shoulder. He snaps his head in a half turn to see the peak of a red cap leaning toward him.

"Please join the group assembling at the start line," an official says softly.

On the track, Gavin grits his teeth and secretly tries to readjust the undercarriage of his shorts that are crimping his testicles. When he raises his head, he is staring into the lens of a CTV camera.

The announcer shifts the crowd's attention from a new attempt at a Canada Games pole vault record to the athletes gathered at the start of the 3,000-metre steeplechase.

With a central starting position in a field of fifteen, Gavin knows he has to get away fast or risk being boxed in. With a good lean, his foot a millimetre behind the line, his opposite arm well in front, he is ready. A subdued murmur descends as the starter raises his orange luminescent-sleeved arm. The wind muffles the pistol's crack. Gavin knifes through to the position he sought, close to the leaders but not in the lead.

As the second-string runner from Ontario, and ranked tenth, Gavin has no illusions of winning. On the other hand, he must spare nothing in scrambling to the finish in the briefest time. Stumbles, furtive glances, and ragged breathing dominate the cluster of the lead athletes.

With two laps to go, Gavin's Ontario teammate bursts out. The pack simmers, debating the wisdom of going after the leader. A Manitoba athlete takes pursuit and stalls one hundred metres later; soon he drifts onto the infield grass to cushion his buckling knees. The main group string out, like boy scouts on a hike, trying to minimize the distance they cover on curves.

Gavin's knees feel like frozen rubber when he hurdles, but still he passes a Herring Choker whose trailing knee brushes an obstacle. GO! A voice screams in Gavin's head. But his insubordinate legs maintain the same cadence. He out-leans a British Columbia athlete for fifth in establishing a personal best of nine minutes 23.4 seconds.

Feeling comfortable minutes later angers him; he realizes he could have pushed harder. He joins the two steeplechasers from British Columbia for a warmdown outside the stadium. When he returns, he adds his Ontario wind suit to his sweat clothes and reclines on a lower bleacher. He has trouble believing the long-awaited race is over. The months of anticipation for nine minutes and some seconds of controlled violence seems peculiar. Yet, in a sense, without the anticipation of a great challenge he feels empty.

The stiff breeze makes him shiver in spite of his clothing. Gavin's muscles now give him the sensation he has portaged a canoe up Mount Robson. Thoughts of a warm shower at residence prompts him to get up. When he does, he sees someone hurrying down the stadium steps two at a time.

"Gavin, what a great race!" Lisa hollers and smothers him in a bear hug.

"Hi there—Lisa, great to see you!"

"Got—in—this—morning, drove from Chapleau," her eyes still bulging with excitement.

Gavin studies this tanned girls arms and legs. She's wearing a white golf shirt with an ocean blue collar. She looks unaware the skin below her denim shorts vibrates with goose pimples. Her hair puzzles him a moment, until he realizes she has had it cut. She's wearing a gold rope chain around her neck.

"What've you been up to this summer?"

"Planted trees May and June; now I'm a cook's helper. I've more pep for training this way; I often get out twice a day."

There was something more about Lisa that Gavin couldn't figure out; finally he realizes she's wearing contact lenses. What happened to that withdrawn girl he knew back at Laurentian, he ponders.

"Where are Tanya and Scott?"

"Probably resting. They both compete soon and they're supposed to keep out of the sun," Gavin mentions in a voice that lacks conviction.

"You mean they didn't see your race?"

"Don't know, I haven't seen either of them at the meet. Tanya and I haven't connected since we got here, and I stayed away from Scott; he's in his hate the opposition mood."

Lisa wrinkles her forehead and then with a strange smile says, "Maybe we should celebrate your race."

Gavin looks at her with beaming eyes, but another gust of wind makes his lips tremble, "Sure—where do you—you suggest we go?"

"Let me drive you back, we'll figure something out on the way."

Chapter 15

"Let's try the Pagoda Gardens; that's if you still like Chinese food," Lisa pauses to exchange smirks and adds, "We might check the action in Waverly Park after that, see you at eight?"

"Sounds good," Gavin says and gently closes her sagging Volkswagen door. He strides to the control gate but halts when he sees Tanya standing in front of him. Tanya is talking with a grey-haired gentleman.

Sensing someone behind her, Tanya turns; her face reddens, "Hi—ah—hi," she utters and swallows hard. "Dad, I would like you to meet Gavin."

"Gavin, this is my father, Reginald Thoburn."

"Well, for goodness sake, I've heard so much about you," Thoburn replies in the voice of a radio announcer.

"Dad's down for my race tomorrow."

"Terrific!" Gavin says, but his feet keep shuffling.

"Couldn't get to your race. How did you do?"

"Oh my God, Tanya, you should've told me."

"It's okay Dad; they suggested we keep out of the sun."

"That so?" They both turn eagerly to Gavin.

"Didn't get a medal but did all right. How you managing Mr. Thoburn?"

"I've been walking regularly, even starting to jog—say, why don't we go for a cola?"

Tanya looks coolly at Gavin.

"Let's see, —ah—" Gavin checks his Casio, "sure I have time."

After ordering, Gavin asks, "Did you drive out, Mr. Thoburn?"

"Why, yes, and we saw the Big Nickel in Sudbury, a female black bear with two cubs near Marathon, and a cow moose on the outskirts of Thunder Bay. I caught the bears on my Leica. It wasn't tiring, Joyce did the driving."

Tanya's jaw drops, and she blinks repeatedly.

Turning to Tanya, Thoburn says, "You remember McPherson's chalet on the point past the bridge closest to our cottage?"

Tanya relaxes her face and forces a smile, "Yes, I think so."

"Anyway, I mentioned at a Property Owner's meeting that you were competing in Thunder Bay; she offered to drive out and visit her aunt."

Pushy—Tanya figures, she stares at her fizzing ginger ale.

Thoburn, noticing Gavin rotating his glass, says, "We won't keep you Gavin."

Tanya's dad drives them back, kisses Tanya, and promises to find her in the warmdown area after her race next day.

During the short wait at the security check Tanya asks, "Will you join me in a walk, I'm restless?"

When Gavin checks his watch, Tanya asks, "Do you have other plans?"

"I'm free for an hour before meeting Lisa."

After Tanya squints, Gavin adds, "Remember Lisa from Laurentian, she popped over for my race."

"Oh, Lisa made it. Good!" Tanya replies nonchalantly but she can't conceal a stagnant stare. She wonders how Lisa, the girl who moped around with the energy of a spent battery, could ever muster the spunk to befriend Gavin so quickly. Then with a cracking voice says, "No, don't change your plans."

Gavin hesitates; he tries making eye contact. But Tanya, who fears bursting into tears, avoids looking at him. Gavin waits another few seconds, places his hand on her shoulder, and says, "Good luck tomorrow, your solid training will put you right in there."

"Thanks, see you," Tanya whispers and twists quickly away. She heads down a long walkway. A day ago she ditched Fred when his celebratory stupor after his sailing victory stretched into its third day. And now, Gavin has other interests.

As Tanya walks, each new outburst of laughter jabs at Tanya's concentration on her race. She thinks that everyone is having fun but her. But then the frequency of guffaws springing from open windows convinces her that more than just the winners are tilting glasses. Commiserating with each other in defeat is also celebrated she figures, and wonders why she has a heavy heart. It's all a lot of fun. She stops, sits on a park bench, and deliberates for several minutes. She returns to her room and digs out the seed times of her rivals.

Ranked seventh discourages her but she remembers with a coy smile coach Tanner's words, "Seed times mean little when only half achieve their best in actual Games." Tanya leaves the room she shares with three other girls and walks down a secluded way in back of residence.

In passing one of the open windows at the recreational wing, she identifies Johann Strauss's "Blue Danube" rising from the ground floor windows. When she gets closer, she peeks in the open curtain of a small chapel and gawks in disbelief. Scott, alone, sways to the rhythm he creates caressing the keys.

The next day while Lisa and Gavin sit high in the stadium waiting for Tanya's race Lisa asks, "What happened to you two?"

"She met a guy she knew on the sailing team and we drifted," Gavin says in an indifferent tone.

Lisa senses more for she noted a strange gaze in Gavin's eyes.

On the track, Tanya looks casual and stays close to the rear of the pack the first three laps. In the stands, Gavin clenches his teeth wondering if she hadn't let the field get too far ahead. Gavin feels ashamed as earlier he had secretly hoped she wouldn't match his success. Finally, with two laps to go and after Tanya has steadily crept closer to the leaders, Gavin climbs on top of his bleacher seat and screams for Tanya to pick off the athletes whose knees have jellied. Gavin and Lisa smack palms when Tanya swerves ahead of the third positioned athlete before the finish. Her time of nine minutes 32 seconds betters her previous best by eighteen seconds.

After the last event Lisa mentions, "It's Quebec Day at Waverly Park this evening. They have traditional and modern entertainers. What do y' say we go?"

Gens du Pays rings through the night air. When the performers call on those assembled to join, Lisa shocks Gavin by not only knowing the words but by singing so confidently that she leads those surrounding. It reminds Gavin of childhood New Year's Eve parties at Grand'mère Vernier's when Uncle Jacques would play his accordion and all would sing.

Late that evening Gavin quietly makes his way to the residence control point. A tall burly, security guard, well into pensionable age, puts down his steaming cup of tea to demand, "Now where might you be expectin' to go at this time of the night?" He shoves a delinquency register in Gavin's face with the Ontario Chef-de-Mission's name on it. "Sign here laddie and settle it directly with your boss."

Gavin dutifully signs but smiles inwardly at the contrast from last week when he walked through holding swimming heat sheets for Cynthia. Quietly he enters his dark dormitory room. He leaves the door ajar so he can see from the hall lights. As he undresses he hears throaty breathing from the others assigned to this room. Except for Scott, who stares and mumbles at the bunk above him.

"How you doing Scott?" Gavin whispers.

"Ready! Ready, for those bastards."

Gavin glares at Scott, remains motionless and sighs. He says softly, "Scott, they're athletes like us. They're okay!"

"No, they're crap! You have to hate them to beat them. There's no other way!"

"But Tanner told us it's best to concentrate on our own performance."

Scott doesn't reply. He puts on a sweatsuit and a pair of training shoes and heads out the door. Gavin follows.

"Scott, wait up," Gavin calls in the corridor.

Across the hall, someone abruptly opens a door. A short stocky man, clad in white wrinkled shorts with a too long drawstring, growls, "You! What do you think you're doing? Cut the bloody noise!" He immediately darts his black, curly-haired body back in the room but not before disturbing every sleeping moth in the hallway.

Scott clenches his fist and makes a move to reopen the door. Gavin grabs Scott's arm and leads him to the recreation area.

When they are seated Scott says, "I have to do well. My old man has been telling everyone at the station that I'm a cinch to win and if I don't, I'll never hear the end of it."

"Scott, you can only do your best."

"Ah, bull shit! You've got to come up with a super performance in the biggest meet of the year. That's the sign of a real athlete and that's what I plan on doing."

"Okay, good luck!" Gavin says and stands up and leaves. When he crawls into his Ontario Team issued sleeping bag, his zest for Scott's success diminishes.

After the last track event, Lisa offers Gavin a ride to Chapleau. Having never driven through that part of Ontario, Gavin agrees. He receives permission to travel on his own and sells his return air ticket to the spouse of an archery competitor from Sudbury.

On the eastern outskirts of Thunder Bay Lisa pulls over at an Amethyst Factory. "Gavin," Lisa says, "I want you to have a memento of your race. These amethyst rocks, more precisely amethystine quartz, have a purple colour caused from low level radioactivity on the iron they contain." Lisa picks up Gavin's gift she has ordered and hands it to him.

Gavin unwraps the penholder embedded in an amethyst crystal and holds it to the sunlight and says, "Who knows what magic lurks in the heart of these crystals?"

Lisa convinces Gavin to make a small detour to visit the Ouimet Canyon. She swerves her way up the curvy road. On the bench overlooking the main lookout, Lisa removes a cloth from a picnic shoulder bag and unwraps a wedge of Swiss cheese.

"The hike gave us a chance to stretch," Gavin says, before he munches into the fresh bread.

"I guess the Canyon wasn't too much after all," Lisa says and unwraps a bottle of Bella Spumante with a couple of plastic glasses. After filling two she hands one to Gavin and stands with arm raised, "To the Canada Games and all the Games to follow."

It was midnight when they turned off Highway 17 at Wawa and after 2:00 a.m. when Lisa pulled into her driveway on Lansdowne North in Chapleau.

"Guess everyone is at our camp on Seven Mile Lake."

"Why don't I unroll my sleeping bag here?" Gavin says when they walk through the large screened front porch.

"As you wish, there's no shortage of beds upstairs; it wouldn't take a minute to set one up."

Gavin drops his sleeping bag on the couch.

He couldn't figure what woke him next morning for he became conscious of a robin's chirping and a warm body next to his at the same instant.

When he shifts to more comfortably fit Lisa into his unzipped sleeping bag, she whispers, "Gavin, I must be back at the tree planting camp by noon. We don't have much time."

Gavin stretches for his socks at the sound and smell of frying bacon.

"Would you like to try some fried wild mushrooms? My mother and I picked these the last weekend I was home and we froze them. They're called *boletus mirabilis*; we've been eating them for years."

"Great."

Gavin watches Lisa take her first mouthful before he tries the yellow and tan mushrooms with bacon. As Lisa clears the table Gavin wonders about Tanya. He hadn't done anything but extend a congratulatory handshake after her race.

When Lisa notices Gavin's reflective mood, she says, "Gavin, the shortcut through Sultan is your best bet; I will make a map and take you to a good hitchhiking intersection on Highway 127."

With his red Ontario sweat top and his two bags with Canada Games emblems, Gavin has no trouble hitchhiking back to Sudbury.

Chapter 16

Although Chapleau youngsters have always idolized high profile sportspeople, Lisa has never known anyone who has practised his or her sporting activity essentially all year. Seeing Gavin's progress at the Canada Games, and experiencing a thirty-seven second drop in her own best run over a five-kilometre bush circuit, instills in her fresh faith in the effectiveness of lengthy preparation.

Back at Laurentian, she badgers Gavin with questions: "Should I start weight training? Would vitamin pills help? Could my iron level be too low? Am I covering sufficient kilometres per week?"

"Lisa, it's not easy to say," Gavin would initially add lengthy explanations. When Lisa's follow up questions exposed glaring holes in Gavin's logic, his responses become terse. Finally Gavin concedes, "Lisa, I can't tell you why but certain things work, that's enough for me. Talk it over with Tanner and you'll get sounder reasons."

But Lisa continues an avalanche of questions every time they meet. Soon Gavin avoids the places he habitually sees Lisa; her questions provoke doubts that he has trouble functioning under. Without conscious awareness, he shifts more of his attention back to Tanya.

Gavin, Tanya, Scott, and Lisa form the nucleus of the university team working through the fall of 1981 and into 1982. Tanya kicks off the 1982 indoor season with a snappy 800-metre run at the York University Invitational. Three days later, coach Andy Tanner picks up a ringing telephone.

"Hello, Andy, it's Paul Perry calling. Tanya Thoburn sure looked sharp last Saturday; if she's available, I would like to include her in the Canadian Women's 800-metres in the Toronto Star Indoor Games."

"Good, we have nothing planned that weekend."

"What do you figure she can do?"

"She did 2:13 last week; probably go down a couple more seconds."

"Great! That would make her competitive. Will you be with her?"

"Yes."

"I'll leave passes for you both at the Wood Street entrance."

Tanner puts the receiver down, spins his swivel chair, and springs to his feet. He searches for Tanya in the foyer. As the sun rose on a crisp Friday morning, Tanner, Tanya, and three other students in a dodge van swing south at Sudbury's Four Corners. They are on their way to the Toronto Star Indoor Games. Tanya, in between naps in the front seat, smiles musing on her invitation to the Gardens. Outside, the sun's reflection on the iced-covered fields sparkles her passage over the many kilometres. Closer to Toronto, she senses that her success as a runner has neutralized the sting of her parental squabble. It acted on her, she figured, the same way the Georgian Bay winds vibrate encrusted snow from the adjacent conifer boughs.

At 6:00 p.m. Tanya picks up her pass, program, and competitor's number at the Athletes' Entrance. Ghosts of hockey players skate through her mind when she walks along the photograph-enshrined corridor. When the organist strikes up, "Meet me in St. Louis", her eyes moisten, for it was her dad's favourite when the family attended Leaf hockey games. She turns a corner and goes through a partition. A whiff of fresh paint reminds her of other walks down these same corridors. Did she ever imagine that some day she would be competing in Maple Leaf Gardens? After finding the appropriate dressing room, she changes quickly, hoping involvement in her warmup will repress her nostalgia.

During the actual race Tanya doesn't know the number of laps that make up 800 metres on this smaller track. It wasn't until the end of the second lap that she realized the frantically waved numbers by a gentleman in a tuxedo indicated the laps remaining. Tanya by this time has also controlled the wide drift she tended to have after each bend: she learned to lean earlier going into the curves. The scamper around the springy track ends before she shows any sophistication at countering her competitors' moves. She beams at the digital timer at the finish line that flashes two minutes 11.34 seconds for fourth place.

Greedily she sucks air to neutralize her acid-swamped blood. Lightheaded, she consoles herself knowing that this misery will help crank up her speed for future 3,000-metre races. She walks along the warmup corridor at ice level for ten minutes before she remembers that her father had agreed to meet her. On the ground level corridor her gaze settles on a man outside the Hot Stove Restaurant. But this gentleman's open neck plaid shirt, corduroy pants, and moccasin type shoes are not her father's Maple Leaf Game's attire. Then she recognizes the Pierre Cardin shirt she had given him for Christmas many years ago. She quickens her strides toward him.

"What speed!" he says and hugs her.

"Here, have this," he removes the plastic lid opening from a ginger ale and hands it to her, remembering this was her favourite drink after swim meets.

"Dad, how've you been? Are you looking after yourself?"

"What can I say? I follow my prescribed thirty minutes exercise five days a week but still have lots of time for taking photos. Incidentally, I took an excellent shot of your finish and a good one of your off-balance struggle the first bend."

"Great, great—how's the settlement going with mom?"

"Only thing left is the splitting of securities. Say, why don't you join me for dinner?"

"Wonderful, Dad! I'll shower now and meet you here after the last event."

Later, at Fred's Oyster House, while Tanya visits the lady's room, Thoburn's eyes dampen when he recognizes his logo design on the restaurant menu. It was while dining here five years ago, celebrating Tanya's Ontario age-class silver swimming medal, that the logo idea came to him. The design, in turn, was triggered by doodles he made during the swim meet. How ecstatic he and Constance had been that evening and how sad he felt they couldn't share this precious moment. When he sees Tanya approaching, he switches his gaze to the jumping blue flame in the gas fireplace.

On seeing his long face and moistened eyes, Tanya asks, "What's up Dad?"

Shocked he hasn't hidden his grief better, Thoburn replies, "I'm happy for you Tanya, chasing your passion for things you enjoy is certainly the way to live." He pauses to look at a mole on the back of his hand and adds, "When I realized my bosses directed the thrust of my advertising pitch away from the quality of the product and more at the insecurities of the potential buyers, I lost interest in my work. What's more I entered advertising because of my photography skills and ended up doing less and less as I climbed the ladder. I never put it together until I had this attack. I'm sure I made the right decision in leaving. Anyway—what'll you have?"

Tanya gazes at her father in a peculiar way. Could he be saying his career was a mistake? No, all her life she knew he had the perfect job. His firm smothered him with praise. He couldn't have lived a lie. Maybe—she considers with horror—he's had a stroke with his attack and things aren't clicking in his grey cells. When Thoburn registers Tanya's uncomprehending look the pit of his stomach shrinks.

Tanya cringes at his sudden reaction, but then relaxes when she decides that with that perception, he must still have full wattage upstairs. Thankful for her sudden recall of her dad's friend that he had motored to Thunder Bay with last summer, Tanya asks, "What's Joyce up to?"

"Oh, oh, she's back in Buffalo supervising the family funeral business until her eldest son takes over; we haven't been in touch since the summer."

Tanya listens but her mind still struggles with her father's debasement of his life's work.

After dinner Reginald Thoburn returns to his third floor apartment on Kingston Road; he craves a martini but settles for the last ginger ale at the back of the fridge. He clanks the can on the kitchen counter cursing his decision to not stock Johnny Walker any longer. Reginald breaks the can's tab, swears again and uses a can opener.

He settles into a puffy chair by the window. His eyes drift first to a few patches of dirty snow and then to a solitary willow recently delimbed. Without his job, he senses himself as isolated as that stripped tree. When he tilts the can to his lips the sight of his shirt cuff delights him. He feels proud; he no longer pops buttons when he wears this special shirt.

Six weeks of chess and checkers gave him time to realign his life to his terms. And yet, Tanya's accusatory look gnawed at his liver. Would freelancing for Charlie's agency, a course in sports photography from Ryerson, and making a successful bid on a twenty minute publicity video for the City's Recreation Department be enough?

Taking the time to catch certain city happenings with his camera gave him the sort of feeling his previous job no longer provided: a youngster's toboggan ride, a retiree's cross-country skiing lesson, an early morning jogger greeting the sun, or a skater skimming over Grenadier Pond. Though he hadn't accompanied Constance to church in fifteen years, he thanked whatever God there was for his second chance to chase his interests.

He contemplates his loneliness. His past friendship with Francine Brunet petered out on their first date before they ordered dessert. He now realized their affection was bracketed at task-oriented mutual respect.

His shrinking contacts made him all the more determined to keep closer to his daughters. Carolyn surprised him. She had six months steady work as a receptionist in an insurance office, took karate lessons, and invited him regularly for fish casseroles in her apartment. Perhaps, he smirked, it took a parental breakup to provoke her maturity.

Tanya, he recalled, always showed her resourcefulness. When a series of ear infections drove her out of two provincial swim championships, she shifted her interest to university running. Tonight, she scooted around the Gardens like a big shot. Recalling her reaction to the reasons he offered in leaving his job rankles his soul. When he stands, a chill creeps through him; he remembers her strange stare. Let's hope all fish that go with the flow aren't dead, he concludes. He slumps back in his chair and stares at the truncated tree until he dozes off.

Next morning, he starts an easy run over a carefully measured course on the Beach's Boardwalk bordering Lake Ontario. As he runs, the impact of his decision to quit work returns. He senses the ventricles of his heart are throwing in extra strokes when he broods over his daughter's confused look.

At the turning point, he checks his watch and frowns at his excessive speed. The sun breaking through the shore mist warms his face; he nudges his toque higher to accentuate the tingle it gives his perspiring forehead. When his eyes devour the prismatic array of sunlight slanting through shore ice, his disappointment over Tanya evaporates. He is back in control.

Chapter 17

With February freezing rain, Gavin seeks the sanded city streets. But temperatures plummet, forcing him to grope through bursts of exhaust beside motorists' floppy, frozen tires.

By mid-February, the sun's longer and stronger contact gives Gavin hope that he will soon shake his hacking cough. He has the Ontario University Championships in two weeks, his last chance to make the winter Nationals.

With modified corners on its upper corridor, the Sudbury Arena provides a functional, though precariously narrow, training circuit. Ordinarily, Gavin would run a specific distance in a predetermined time interspersed with recovery jogging. On the Monday preceding the big meet, he doubles over coughing half way through the workout.

Tanner interrupts him saying, "That's it for tonight. A cough without a fever may not be serious but there's no use being dumb about it."

Gavin pouts.

"Would your apartment be too dry?" Tanner asks with the vivid stress lines on his brow imparting concern.

"Could be."

"Humidify the air and you'll cut the irritation."

"How, boil a kettle?" Gavin asks raising his hand to trap another barking barrage.

"Get a small electric humidifier, and fill it with water. Otherwise, soak a towel and hang it over the bathtub." Tanner looks helplessly at Gavin a few seconds. He then casts his sad look at the passageway where walking cardiac patients meld with spurting runners.

Tanya, puffing heavily, stops running and says to Tanner, "I've a Student Council meeting at 6:30; I'll head back with Carl after my last repeat."

"Make sure you get some kind of warmdown or you'll get leg spasms; some things can't be rushed, Tanya."

She finishes her last run, puts on her sweat bottoms and then dashes down the back straightaway trying to poke an arm up her sleeve. Tanner shakes his head when he sees her meet Carl and disappear down the far stairwell.

At the Wednesday workout before the Thursday departure, Tanner is more optimistic over Gavin. Except for two grating coughs during his final warmdown, Gavin is back to normal.

Thursday, Tanner stops the Dodge van at the campus rendezvous point. It is 6:30 a.m. On the eastern horizon, a steel blue sky asserts itself. The athletes clamber aboard, their faces covered with toques and scarves.

Gavin enters last, lurches into a grating cough with his first breath of warm air, regains balance, and is embarrassed as he straddles hand luggage and pivots around teammates' knees. He settles on the three, vacant, back continuous seats with a sigh of satisfaction. His overdue English assignment, completed three hours ago, is in Arvo's care, and he has made the bus. Team trips delight him. His spirit craves the racing challenge, and the meal money provides variety to his menu.

A chill sweeps through him after a two-hour nap. He unrolls his sleeping bag along the rear seat and climbs into it during a break in Parry Sound. When the bus leaves, Gavin glances at Tanya. She has a pillow propped behind her neck and listens to what he believes to be a Hagood Hardy tape.

Three hours later Gavin wakes to Tanner's words, "Before we go to our hotel I want you to warm up on the York University track. Wear your spikes and run a few fast sections on the turns."

With a sleep-cleared head Gavin jogs with the others. Whiffs from repairs on the track's polyurethane surface remind him of the new Canada Games track in Thunder Bay and his success there. He joins Tanya negotiating curves at various speeds.

Tanya, while waiting in the lobby of the Carleton Hotel for her room key, asks Gavin, "What are you up to tonight?"

"Not much, don't feel so good with this cough and all."

"Okay, I'll give dad a shout and maybe join him for dinner."

"Good, give him my best."

After Scott receives the room key, Gavin grabs his loosely tied roll and overnight bag and joins him.

Tanya studies Gavin as he moves toward the elevator. At first she thinks he will trip on his untied shoelaces. When she sees his tangled hair and shirt spilling out of his pants, she wonders why he made the trip. Competing with life in such disarray seems senseless to her.

In his room, Gavin draws water for a bath. He feels relaxed, but every two minutes his chest convulses. After a long soaking, he slithers between sheets. A raw throat reminds him he has a carton of milk tucked in his bag. He grins with each swallow.

Scott bursts in an hour later, "What the hell, you in the sack already?" Scott has a lady friend at his side.

"Hi," Gavin replies blinking and sitting up.

"Saw Tanya leaving with that creep from the yacht club she hung around with at the Canada Games."

"Oh yeah?" Gavin says, turning his head sharply toward Scott. Although Gavin stifles further comment, milk curdles in his stomach. He relaxes thinking Mr. Thoburn must be out; but it hits him squarely, Tanya has contacted Langdon. Gavin asks Scott, "What've you in mind tonight?"

"Think I'll take it easy—want to throw well— if I reach seventeen metres it could set me up for selection on the Commonwealth Team." Scott then turns his attention to the rankings in his latest *Athletics* magazine. The freckled coed in a Windsor wind-jacket shrieks with delight when Scott turns to the high jump. Scott and his friend chat about a piano recital at Hart House and leave.

Gavin coughs in bursts in and out of sleep. When the bass drum in the ballroom below starts thumping, he imagines

Tanya living it up with Langdon while he continues staring at the ceiling.

Early next morning Gavin meets Tanner in the hotel coffee shop and joins him. Gavin never knows whether to call him coach, Mr. Tanner, or Sir; as a result, he emphasizes the "Good morning," when he settles into the booth.

Tanner while refilling his cup from the thermos says, "At the meeting last night your seed time got you into the fast section of the final. It goes at one o'clock Saturday."

"Thank God!" Gavin replies. "It'll give me another day's rest."

When Gavin returns to his room, he finds Scott thumbing through the hotel's complimentary *Globe and Mail.* Scott doesn't raise his head when he says, "Thought I'd dodge your cough last night. I stayed with Windsor friends down the hall." Scott folds the extended newspaper at an article on weight lifting. He doesn't budge his corpulent leg straddling the passageway to Gavin's side of the room.

"Sure," Gavin says, steps around Scott's leg and kicks off his shoes. Sleeping most of the day, he only remembers Lisa dropping off apple juice in the afternoon.

Race day morning Gavin limbers up running from his hotel through Queen's Park and then to a snow-free field beside Hart House. His breathing is easier and he is impatient for the race to begin. When Gavin heads back to his hotel, he reflects on big cities. How jammed Bloor Street was the night they drove in. Then he figures with Canada having 27 million people, and a landmass covering 10 million square kilometres it would give an average of less than three people per square kilometre. He smiles thinking that with the concentration of people in Toronto there would always be open spaces in Canada, at least during his lifetime.

At first the hours before the race seem interminable; suddenly, it is time to report. At the track, his muscles tingle in readiness. He consults Tanner for any prerace advice.

"Stay with the leaders from the start," is all Tanner has to say.

Gavin coughs and nods consent simultaneously. He hustles off. His aquamarine eyes look tired peripherally, but their centres scintillate in a way no one has seen for months.

The lead group doesn't take Gavin seriously when he hounds them on the third, fourth, and fifth laps of this seven and one-half lap race. But when Gavin, the slowest seed in the race, nudges shoulders with the survivors of a fast pace at the end of the sixth, he has their respect. Gavin's strike in the last 100 metres gets him past two of the three ahead of him. He is under the qualifying time of three minutes 54 seconds for entry at the Canadian Intercollegiate Championships in Edmonton the following week.

Chapter 18

"Go Gavin!" Tanya shouts when the athletes head into the final 100 metres of the 1,500-metre heat at the Canadian Championships. Her voice has more sympathy than incitement. Gavin has no trace of the fiery spirit he summoned the previous weekend. A glassy stare dominates a frowning face as he struggles to the finish line.

Tanya scowls at a kid beside her who yaps at Gavin, "You'll never make it."

Tanya, then, reflects on the delicacy of reaching a peak; she figures Gavin has robbed himself of any consistency by his helter-skelter living. He works hard, she wouldn't deny, but she can't understand his lack of organization.

Transferring her inability to help Gavin, Tanya does her warmup with a vengeance. With the crack of the pistol, she forges to the lead in the nine-athlete field. Although she set a scorching pace, a Manitoba athlete stays with Tanya and outleans her at the finish. A glum glance at the electronic time display, for second place, blooms into a jaunty smile when Tanya sees nine minutes 11.3 seconds.

The surprise of the meet, however, is Scott Cassidy. He mounts the top level of the victory podium by dethroning the reigning champion. While the President of the University of Alberta loops the gold medal over his head, Scott flushes with glee. His greatest pleasure is in his anticipated call to his dad. With beefy arms raised, he acknowledges the accolades of the Butterdome fans. His blue eyes moisten; he has achieved a major athletic goal by his second university year. Like a child, he wants this moment to remain forever, and in a way he knows it will.

He descends the dais, his gold medal dangling prominently across his chest. When Scott notices his coach and teammates, he rushes over. In minutes the obsession to call his father takes precedence. He scrounges whatever change the group can muster and digs out a Parker ballpoint pen—a gift from his dad. Scott meticulously records the top three finishers' efforts and dashes up the ramp to the public phones. Still breathless, he dials home and gets his father.

Scott deposits the required coins and says, "I won the gold Dad!"

"No kidding."

"Yeah! Did 16.03 to cinch it on my last throw."

"Did you say that heave won it? That's half a metre behind the standard for the Commonwealth Team. I thought you said you were getting in good training. You've got to think internationally, not those Mickey Mouse university standards."

Scott shrivels like a punctured air mattress. He grabs his Parker pen and starts frenetically pressing and releasing the retrieving knob. A knot of wrinkles creases his forehead; he inflates his massive chest, holds a few moments, and suppresses a mighty urge to tear the telephone door from its hinges; he is oblivious to his father's further chatter. When he regains control, his attention focuses on the excitement generated by a young lady in the next booth. She squeals repeatedly as she recounts her high jump victory to her Vancouver family.

After Scott realigns the telephone receiver, he hears, "You can do it Son, but you must work harder. The same way I had to do to get our police tug-of-war team to beat that Detroit gang."

Scott mumbles, "Okay Dad, I'll be home in three weeks for the Easter weekend, see you then." He releases the receiver high above the hook and lets it crash. He shifts his stare from the swaying coiled cord to the results sheet before mangling it.

A twelve-year-old girl, waiting her turn at the booth, ogles the shot put champion who with sunken eyes and crumpled forehead lumbers toward a trashcan.

"Hey Cassidy, Scott Cassidy," a falsetto voice calls from behind an aisle pillar when Scott ditches his refuse.

Scott turns and sees a tall angular man with a cigarette dangling over a russet beard.

"Congratulations on your win!" Scott shakes the offered hand. "I'm Matte Wade, from Pharmaceutical International; we have products you might want to try."

"What kind of products?"

"Just something to maximize your training," Wade says, and adds, "Why don't you see me in room 723 in the Edmonton Inn, North Tower and I'll explain the nurturing my products will do." Wade scribbles his room number on his business card.

Scott recalls Rawlins Martin's experiences and asks, "What time?"

"Anytime. I'll be in all evening."

"I'll think about it; I've an athletes' banquet tonight."

"It's up to you whether you're serious about being the best. If you are, you'll see me."

"I'm not sure that's the type of commitment I'm willing to make." But his father's condemnation of his progress drones in his mind. He knows he has been pushing his body to his maximum and can't currently cope with any increased work. Scott reconsiders and says, "On the other hand, I might consider sampling something."

Wade draws heavily on his cigarette, gives Scott a stealthy glance, and releases smoke slowly through his nostrils. A faint smile spreads across Wade's face when he says, "Sure, we could put you on a mini or a maxi strength cycle; it's up to you. I'm certain, however, once you see what this stuff will do, you'll be anxious to get its full benefits."

"I'll drop around after the banquet."

"I'll be there." Wade says.

Scott hesitatingly walks back to his friends. The sight of Gavin holding a hamburg for him in the distance makes Scott forget Wade.

Throughout the banquet, Scott's thoughts jump back to Wade. Perhaps that's my answer; a few months on something would surely get me there. His preoccupation with Wade keeps him from savouring the many glasses of Niagara Red Wine he drinks with his roast buffalo. Even more surprising is his lack of reaction to the zesty disco beat on the dance floor. He slips away from Tanya, Gavin and Tanner early.

"Yes," Wade was saying, "these products are the most recently synthesized. Detecting them is impossible, it takes researchers six months to develop a new test. They're a little more expensive but entirely safe." Scott looks at the label, then at the bottle and opens the cover.

"Of course if you want the old stuff, you can stop a month early and it should clear; it's a bit cheaper and seems reliable."

Scott brings the bottle of new capsules under the table lamp; he still can't see well so he grabs a fresh towel from Wade's bathroom rack and shakes out a few. They seem the same as any others. "How much do you take?" Scott asks.

"That depends on how quickly you want to get strong." Wade pauses to rhythmically tap the end of a Camel on the dresser top and stuffs it in his mouth. He lights it, draws a deep breath, and in a bored way continues, "Most athletes start taking 20 mg a day and build from there."

Scott uses all his money for a two-week supply. Wade provides the telephone number of his Toronto distributor. Scott returns to his room and dumps the bottle in his massive left hand. He hesitates as he lifts a tablet to his lips. After pondering the stories on liver cancer, Scott assures himself they can't be worse than women taking birth control pills. He remembers Rawlins saying, "The body's amazing recovery powers can easily adapt to a little biochemical juggling." It'll only be for three months. They mustn't be that bad or they wouldn't make them for humans. Scott swallows one and then another. He is now sure he has the answer to making the 1982 Commonwealth Games Team.

Scott considers evasive tactics should he be challenged. He doesn't trust Wade's promise of complete safety if tested, but he does remember Rawlins talking about a friend at a National Collegiate track meet. This discus thrower, when summoned to report within the hour for a urine test, voided his urine.

Then in the back seat of a van, he had his student-nurse girl friend use a reverse catheter to fill his voided bladder with her urine. At least it fooled the testers in Nebraska.

During his months on steroids, Scott's body weight rises from 90 to 96 kg. He feels confident for he has increased all his personal best lifts. Anxiously he awaits the Commonwealth Games Trials in Ottawa. To be doubly safe, under Wade's advice, he stops taking anything four weeks before the trials. By this time, his outlay for steroids has included money borrowed from his younger brother's university fund. This was done under the guise of special protein supplements.

"No problem," he reassures his brother, "Sports Canada cheques will resolve everything soon."

Chapter 19

With a heave of 17.35 metres Scott places second in the shot at the Summer Nationals in Ottawa. This distance betters the standard for Brisbane in October. With heavy training and steroids Scott adds sixty centimetres. Whether he could have done so on his own will always be a mystery.

A tremor creeps up and down Scott's spine as each well-wisher approaches. He senses sooner or later someone will challenge his camouflage.

In the same trials, Tanya places third and makes the team in the 3,000-metres. Gavin's second place finish in the 3,000-metre steeplechase leaves him nothing more interesting to think about than clearing cross-country ski trails. The committee used each of the top three finishers' overall ranking in the Commonwealth as the selection criteria.

Scott returns to steroids and heavy training from his summer base in Windsor. He stops taking Metandren in September to be clear by the Games in October.

In Australia, a spirited wind ruffles the tranquil city of Brisbane. In the Games Village, located at Griffith University, a composed Tanya is gradually drawn into a flurry. The movie star status she expected collapsed with the assignment of three nervous athletes to the same room. Tanya feels alienated during workouts, as the Canadian distance coach is the personal coach of the other two runners in her event. Although Scott has played several games of chess with her on the flight over, he remains aloof in the village. With dress uniforms delayed in transit, Canadian athletes miss their flag raising ceremony on Village arrival. But even more important to Tanya, she realizes how much she misses Gavin.

It takes the opening ceremonies to ignite Tanya into flames of joy. While the Canadian Team stands in loose formation outside the stadium, Tanya's darting eyes attempt to relate each country's colour and style of outfit with its historic tradition. This sight, more than anything she has experienced, bonds her to these diverse peoples who have had their cultures shaped through having a common British heritage.

Tanya beams when dozens of children enter the marsupial pouch of a thirteen metres tall, motorized kangaroo. What will these kids do, she wonders, with those mini trampolines they clasp so tightly? She regrets the athletes will miss the children's show; she promises herself to catch it on television later.

The incessant winds whipping the Queen Elizabeth II Stadium do little to squelch the braggadocio reverberating in the 60,000, predominantly local, spectators. "Shine on Brisbane" is the city's motto.

Tanya learns that Brisbane was formally discovered in 1824 when Lieutenant John Oxley of the Royal Navy landed in a search for water. It served as a penal colony until it gained civil status in 1842. A puritanical touch, perhaps a reaction to its earlier history, led to the local censoring of certain *Playboy* and *Penthouse* issues as well as gambling machines.

Tanya finds it exciting running over short-cropped grass fields wearing shorts during a time of year she associates with snowfalls and heavy sweatsuits. Race day, she is ready.

On the fourth of October, seventeen athletes report for the final of the women's 3,000-metres. Tanya lacks the experience and confidence to hold her own in the tightly packed group. At the start, an athlete sporting a red rose on her competitive vest forces through a maze of runners. In doing so she nudges Tanya off-stride. Tanya, in turn, strikes the heel of a New Zealand runner. Tanya's remorse doubles when the Kiwi stumbles and shoots a nasty glance back at Tanya. It takes Tanya two laps to exonerate herself of any wrongdoing and refocus on the race. She is gaining at the end but has to settle for sixth place in nine minutes 12.78 seconds.

In Brisbane the cafeteria meals allow Scott to pack in lots of steaks; he also drinks litres of orange juice. He easily maintains his acquired bulk. When the final in the shot arrives, the ninth of October, he is ready.

He heaves 17.23 metres for second place. The exuberance he had in last March's indoor meet in Edmonton with a mere 16.03 metres is gone. His wan smile conceals a stomach infested with a slimy serpent. Scott relaxes when he learns only the winner and the third place finishers receive drug-reporting cards. With the prodigious feat of a silver medal, Scott has no interest in calling home. He even declines an invitation by the Canadian throwing coach to try Australian suds. Instead, that evening, he sits for hours alone in the noisy athletes' lounge sipping a cola drink and reflecting on what he has done. Eventually, he takes a shuttle downtown. He meets guys with red maple leaf jackets and follows them into the Jungle Bar. There he shares jokes but sought, without success, some idle comment that would convince him others on the team resorted to his strength-training strategy.

Chapter 20

Geologists now support the theory that a crashing celestial body formed the crater known as the Sudbury basin. Earlier thinking suggested rising molten masses, some hundreds of millions of years ago, brought valuable minerals to the surface. Whatever its origin, ore in Sudbury attracted the adventuresome. Many brought their sporting traditions with them; others developed new interests to match the untamed environment.

Youngsters of all nationalities maximized the cold temperatures to skate on wild ice and popularized freestyle hockey. With technology came indoor ice surfaces.

Years later, Sudburians were able to capitalize on the perfection of polyurethane as a resilient running and jumping surface. This came in the development of track and field facilities at Laurentian University to host the 1974 Ontario Summer Games. The staging of National and International Championships in the city followed as excitement for track escalated.

On a Monday evening in mid-October many of the track and field enthusiasts in the city gathered at the airport to welcome the return of the local participants from the '82 Commonwealth Games.

On hearing the pilot cut the engines on the Boeing 737, coach Andy Tanner, Gavin and Lisa move toward the arrival area. A ramp truck sidles up to the plane's belly.

Scott, at the top of the ramp, smiles when he spots the gang at the reception area. He retrieves his silver medal and dangles it from his neck.

A bronzed Tanya, in her powder blue, team blazer, radiates to the welcoming group her stored Brisbane sunshine. When she descends, a breeze teases blond strands across her face.

Lisa, who watched every available track and field telecast on the Commonwealth Games, keeps fidgeting. She fires such a barrage of idolized chatter that there isn't a person in the airport waiting room who doesn't know something special is happening.

Tanya greets her friends with smiles, hugs and a good word for each. Scott appears happy, but the expected glow after a stellar performance isn't there. Gavin with a suppressed smirk wonders if it's because Scott has yet to recover from three days of celebrating.

Tanner, when probing the possible reasons behind Scott's summer breakthrough, receives only evasive answers. Scott, earlier, would provide the minutest of details to anyone who asked. A puzzled Tanner recalls how Scott returned to Windsor after final exams and trained on his own except for weekly visits to a throws' coach in Toronto. Tanner wonders was it an alteration in his technique or a sudden strength breakthrough. Moments later, in observing Scott retrieve his luggage, Tanner gawks at Scott's bulkiness. The pernicious thought of steroids sizzles through Tanner's mind. Tanner scratches his bushy mustache but relaxes on remembering Scott's convincing condemnation of steroids during a conversation last February.

After the fanfare at the airport and the drive into Sudbury, Tanner drops Tanya, Gavin, and Scott at the University Residence. Gavin shoulders Tanya's giant duffle bag.

In the elevator Gavin urges Tanya for details of her race: intermediate times, position each lap, finishing kick, and the weather during her event. Gavin gleams with pride sharing her experiences though harbouring a speck of envy. Once in the room they hug in silence for several seconds.

"The trip was fantastic," Tanya says softly, "but there were times before the competition when everyone was up tight. At that time, I thought it wasn't worth it. After my race I went sightseeing and loafed on a beach. It was strange thinking how the city started as a penal colony. The mayor of Brisbane was drunk with pride every time he spoke; he even claimed he would go after future Olympic Games."

Tanya unzips her largest bag and removes several items: two white caps with maple leaf emblems, three Canadian T-shirts, two golf shirts, two sweatsuits, a boomerang, and a rugby shirt.

When Gavin's eyes bulge at the sight of the rugby shirt, Tanya says, "Try it on, it's too big for me."

When he does, and it fits, Tanya says, "It's yours."

"But I can't … Thanks, it's great!" Gavin gives her arm a gentle squeeze. On returning to his room, a couple of hours later, Gavin can't wait for his next practice.

The Monday after the Ontario University Outdoor Championship, Coach Tanner calls a team meeting. He says, "We have to point for the Ontario Indoor Championship in Windsor the first weekend in March and then the Nationals in Toronto. For a few of you, there'll be Montreal trials in late June for the World University Games taking place in Edmonton next summer. For Scott and Tanya, I don't want to see you for three weeks but keep active. The rest are on your own for a week and then we get down to business."

And business it was, for Gavin was able to join the other two on Canada's National Team for the World Universiade in Edmonton.

Though boycotts plagued the University Games, 3,500 athletes from 74 countries competed in 10 sports. It was the largest International Games next to the Olympics. Track and field maintained its traditional focal point. The ambience created by the Edmontonians and the astute officiating allowed the diverse students of the world the chance to compete with the least controversy.

The seven days before his event, Gavin trains on the ravine trails close to the Athletes' Village at Lister Hall. In this way, he avoids the hype of the Games. He rooms with Scott. Early each morning, he runs before breakfast. Later his workout is on the university track or nearby grass fields.

With the coolness of an experienced canoeist in white water, he races the seven lap 80 metre distance of the 3,000-metre steeplechase against the toughest university athletes in the World. His no-frills, even-paced race earns him a fifth spot, and convinces him that he can make it to the top eventually. When Gavin returns to his room after his race, he notices the cleaning lady has placed a sheet of blue paper relating to Metandren dosages on his desk. He picks it up and reads, "Take three tablets (30 mg) two hours before and two tablets (20 mg) after a workout. Allow tablets to dissolve under the tongue; twice the dosage must be given if swallowed to allow for the lack of absorption." What was this substance anyway? Metandren—never heard of it—then he shoots his arms in the air and clutches the sides of his head. He feels as if he has opened someone else's mail. He plops on a chair before his rubbery legs lose their support. It can't be, he says to himself; he sits in a daze for an hour.

On hearing the room lock open behind him, Gavin breaks out of his trance.

It is Scott who says, "Hey, good going kid, you had a great race!" Scott gives Gavin a couple of congratulatory pats on the back.

"Yeah, thanks, I was happy about it," Gavin replies in a monotone; Gavin has a flash thought to keep quiet—but he can't. "Ah...ah...ah...Scott," Gavin stands and hands Scott the blue sheet which was on his desk. "Is this yours?"

Scott scans the blue paper; his face blanches while his eyes electrify, "Where did you get this?"

Gavin collapses back in his chair, tosses his head over the backrest and closes his eyes.

"Tell me where you got this or I'll—."

Gavin remains still, his fingers interlocked pleading with every God he ever knew to tell him this wasn't happening. He takes a deep breath, then letting air out slowly between his clenched teeth says, "Somebody, ... probably the cleaning lady, put it on my desk!"

Scott sighs, gasps twice, pauses, and then stares directly at Gavin. Although Scott's lips twitch as if formulating a statement, he says nothing. Instead he returns his gaze to the wastebasket. The place, he now figures, he should have thrown Matte Wade's sheet the first day he saw it.

After four minutes of silence Gavin stands, loops his identification card over his ears, rotates his head back and forth and while staring at Scott says, "What a chicken shit way to compete!"

Although Scott hasn't taken steroids for a month, he has forgotten about tucking this sheet in his training diary several weeks ago. It must have dropped, he figured, when he hurriedly put his log away when Gavin returned unexpectedly early from his race-day easy morning run.

Gavin walks toward the cafeteria at Lister Hall. He has eaten only a bowl of porridge and toast with jam this morning, yet he has no zest for food. Questions keep reverberating in his head. Why would Scott do this when his training was going so well? When had he started? What would happen if he got caught? Is it up to me to squeal? Gavin walks down the street overlooking the ravine and across the grass boulevard. He wonders how someone, so close, could stoop to this? Gavin would like to share his misery with Tanya, but she competes tomorrow. He decides the best thing is to tell Tanner. But, he thinks, Scott may be only considering it. Perhaps the sheet belonged to a friend. He can't accuse him if he hasn't seen him take the stuff. Dope control has to handle it. But Scott's reaction was not that of an innocent man, he reminds himself. Finally, his rumbling stomach guides him back to the residence cafeteria.

Gavin winces the next day at the stadium when he sees Scott warming up for the shot. How can a person cheat in a competition in which pride of achievement is the main reward? Could the flush of glory mask the ice corroding the performer's heart? Until yesterday, drug users were the other guys, the lower echelon, the untouchables; today that net included his former friend. He wonders how he could have been so naive. With watery eyes he watches the brazen Scott take his preliminary throw. A tall Canadian 400-metre hurdler seated in front of Gavin remarks flippantly, "Take a look at the beef out there, half those guys are on 'roids."

The hurdle's coach seated beside the athlete replies, "Scott sure isn't getting any thinner."

Gavin remains in stony silence. A day ago he would have verbally mauled a person making such an accusation.

Scott places third. Gavin leaves, not waiting for the victory ceremony. At the far end of the stadium his gaze catches the list of names of financial supporters for this track built for the '78 Commonwealth Games. He shakes his head. Then he casts a sad glance at the many track and field officials who gave up so many fishing trips so athletes could compete with as much impartiality as was practical—and then this.

Killing time before Tanya's event, Gavin strolls downtown. He trudges for three hours mulling over what would lead an athlete to stoop to this level.

Gavin returns to the stadium to see Tanya's race. She lets the seven leaders chew each other up with a fast initial pace. Then she moves past three exhausted athletes to claim fourth. It seems to Gavin that Tanya lacked the resilience to recover after going flat out two days earlier in order to qualify for the final.

That evening when Scott returns to residence with his medal, Gavin doesn't speak to him. He ignores the mournful eyes of his roommate who sought verbal petting.

Chapter 21

Scott becomes a Sports Canada "C" carded athlete. A nine hundred and fifty-dollar cheque appears in his mailbox every second month. He can also claim up to three thousand dollars on training or travel expenses. He stays with the same plan for 1984. Around the university he and Gavin don't even grunt when they pass each other.

Shocked when this rift continues between his two outstanding male athletes, Tanner asks Gavin at the end of practice one day, "What's up between you two?"

"He's gone big time on me, needs to belittle his opponents to psych himself up; I'm tired of him; that approach sickens me; I'd quit rather than do that."

"Oh, I see," Tanner replies, "I'll talk to him. Is there anything else?"

Gavin shrugs, thinking what else can he say.

Tanya takes a month off training instead of the coach's recommended three-week switch of physical activities. She accepts the vice-presidency of the Student's General Association. Then, having skimped on her gradual build up, she returns directly to hard running. This causes an irritation on the sole of her foot the trainer calls plantar fasciitis. Three weeks later when the condition lingers she withdraws from the team's roster.

At seven-thirteen in the evening on a Friday, a year and a half later in Winnipeg, Scott wins the 1984 Olympic Trial shot put. His performance betters the Canadian Olympic Association's standard—a more severe requirement than that set down by the International Amateur Athletic Federation. Scott has barely time to tuck his medal in his sports bag before his presence is requested at drug control.

In the same trials, Gavin wins the steeplechase in Canadian record time. His performance, however, doesn't rank in last year's world top sixteen. The Canadian Olympic Committee does not select him. Gavin reproaches himself for not going faster but bristles at the thought his country imposes a standard more severe than that requested by the international group controlling the Los Angeles Olympics.

Tanner, on the flight back to Sudbury, watches Gavin snap the pages of a *MacLean's Magazine* the way a bank teller cracks each bill in counting a stack of twenties. He sighs, and vows he will apply for the advertised full-time track and field position as Canadian technical coordinator in Ottawa. It's time, he decides, someone working from the inside straightens out Games' selections.

"Remember, Gavin," Tanner says, "Los Angeles is only one meet; don't lose your momentum. Your training is right; the system's working."

Gavin frowns, stops flicking pages, shifts his heavy eyes to Tanner and says, "I'll take a break before I decide."

"Just remember you've reached an incredible level, if your fitness withers you might never recapture it; keep active."

Gavin stares blankly up the aisle of the aircraft. Although he wouldn't admit it to Tanner, winning in Canadian record time infuses rapture in every synapse of his nervous system. Triple five thousand training heart beats each day would still be worth the chance to tingle this way again.

Andy Tanner's first letter the next day is to the Canadian Olympic Committee. He points out how current performance is not an appropriate assessment of a season's best. World rankings are made at the end of the season. Could Gavin's omission have been a misjudgment?

"No," the president replies, "merely a tightening of standards."

In Windsor, after his glorious weekend, Scott appears on two television and three radio interviews in two days. The Police bulletin board displays every newspaper version of his exploits. In the lunch room at the main station Captain Cassidy explains, "I told Scott he had to shift his thinking to international standards and go all out; my God he had the balls to do it."

"Yes, Captain, that son of yours showed what Windsor lads are made of," Sergeant Wentworth chimes in while studying a newspaper photo of Scott's winning put.

A few kilometres away on Cabana Road, Scott rose from his dad's easy chair to answer the telephone. He has been rereading a stack of newspaper articles about his achievements. Expecting a lengthy call, Scott brings a tumbler of orange juice with him. He smiles as he lifts the receiver, "Good morning, Scott Cassidy speaking."

The Canadian Track and Field technical coordinator, after exchanging greetings, says, "Scott, your drug test is positive!"

Scott topples his juice; it gushes over the counter and drips on the floor. Scott sidesteps the mess and slowly presses the receiver back to his ear. He grunts at each statement.

After the call, Scott racks his brain for an explanation. Surely Wade hadn't flubbed on that supposedly new substance. Scott verifies from the blue sheets and his training journal that what he followed was accurate. His jaw twists and his eyeballs bulge; his right fist punches his left palm like the piston of a locomotive.

News of Scott's disqualification sweeps the Windsor area three times faster than his victory. Captain Cassidy seeks refuge from the media in his home each lunch hour. The Cassidy telephone lines remain unplugged except for outgoing calls.

Three days later, via registered mail, Scott is invited to witness the second test to verify the earlier findings. He studies the letter for hours. The sport to which he dedicated so much of his life has rejected him. What could he do without shot putting, he asks himself. This pesters him. Then something strange hits him. In going over his training journal, he realizes that the dream of being the best in the world every time he picked up a shot had lost its sting. His passion had eroded. He further notices the frequency and details of his training entries shifted from technique in the shot circle and weight room to pharmaceutical jottings. Skill analysis was abandoned six months ago. A year and a half has passed without his recording of a single training objective.

He declines the invitation and applies the same day to transfer into an art's program at the University of Windsor. His mother smiles when she sees him dust off the piano. He notices his old music sheets appear from nowhere. His father interrupts his recent preoccupation of staring out the rear window at his bird feeder to help Scott move the piano back upstairs.

In Sudbury, Gavin clears brush from ski trails at minimum wage. After work he goes for token runs over the same paths. But he lumbers on routes he earlier dashed over.

As controversy rages in the Canadian media over selection of Canada's Track Team, Gavin's hopes soar. Many petitions demand selection of athletes who have achieved the International Standard. The Canadian Olympic Committee finally reconsiders and adds five athletes. Gavin is not amongst those added. Deflated once again, he curses the Canadian Olympic Committee with every stroke of his machete for eight hours a day.

Taking a sauna, one week before the start of the Olympics, Gavin overhears two older gentlemen talking. "I wish I could find one or two people to join me on my drive to L. A. now that you're not going Frank," a tall grey-haired man remarks. This man spoke through fingers that protected his face from the sizzle instigated after his partner doused the baking rocks.

Frank replies, "I'd sure love to catch the swimming; our boy Baumann could pick up all the marbles; but I have a camp on Lake Panache and promised the family to build a dock. Ah hell Percy, why don't you fly?"

Percy exhales slowly, rubs perspiration from around a large mole at the back of his neck, turns to Frank, and says, "Costs more than a thousand bucks and you don't get a feel for the country. I also want to take a few slides for my geography classes. I like having my own vehicle. Renting is expensive and a pain in the ass."

Gavin listens intently and makes some mental calculations. Since he is on the Ontario athletes' support program, he doesn't have to worry about tuition; the money he has saved could tide him over for his other expenses. He can also return to work after the Games. Why not ask?

Frank, who has reneged on the trip, gets down once more and hoses water on the rocks. He lets out a sigh when the scalding wave shivers him, "Geez, I would love to join you Percy, a trip across the U.S. would be fascinating, but not this year."

Percy doesn't respond. He concentrates on keeping the heat from his face with his hands.

After a long pause, Gavin clears his throat, hesitates while a sharp cracking sound from the baking rocks loses its startle, and says, "Did I hear you right? Are you looking for someone to go with you to the Games?"

"That's right! You're with the track team aren't you?"

"Yes," after the heat sears his face once more, Gavin adds, "How much do you figure it would cost?"

"If you're willing to share the driving, I'll cover the car expenses. Come to a few hundred I guess for meals and accommodation and a fair amount for tickets depending on how many events you take in."

"Sounds interesting. I'd like to join you, if I may?"

"Sure, I'm Percy Gibb on Ramsey Lake Road."

Gavin sees his face clearly for the first time, " I'm Gavin Gosling. I remember helping you at a swim meet for my aquatics course. You were chief timer." Gavin never forgot his aquatics instructor extolling the virtues of people like Mr. Gibb who through their enthusiasm for officiating made amateur sports happen.

"Glad you're interested. I'll be leaving early Thursday. Give me a call if you have any questions."

When Mr. Gibb leaves the sauna, Gavin notices his bushy, grey eyebrows and his deep-lined face. A man, Gavin muses, who has seen much of life's fortunes and tribulations but who still chases excitement.

On Thursday Gibb arranges a foam mattress over the collapsed back seat of his Coronet station wagon. A cardboard box next to his flight pack contains library books on Michigan, Wisconsin, Iowa, Nebraska, Colorado, New

Mexico, and California. Loose beside the propped-up cushion is a recent copy of *Sports Illustrated* and two copies of *Canadian Swimming.*

When Gavin is driving, Gibb reclines with his head elevated. He offers snippets of interest on early settlers or geographic features of the surrounding area. Every so often he requests Gavin to pull over so he can photograph an historic town hall or a certain stratification of rock. Being an ex-swimmer, Gibb completes a thirty-minute hike sometime in the day. This suits Gavin who heads for the less frequented side roads for his maintenance run.

In Iowa, Gibb pulls off Interstate 80 to photograph a mobile one hundred-metre corn irrigation arm mounted on wheels. Gavin, while he drives through the night, dodges shredded rubber and stricken animals. A particular rabbit has stiffened limbs raised as if in defiance to its assaulter. At dawn, Gavin's itchy eyes prompt him to open the air vent. The scent of freshly mown hay braces him for another hour before Gibb takes over.

At noon they head south on Interstate 25 through Colorado. The next time Gavin raises his eyelids he sees a sign for Santa Fe. Did cowboys and stagecoaches use this route?

In the remote areas again and fully awake, Gavin ponders the lifestyles of people who clung to homes under relentless winds and scorching suns. He thinks of Louis l'Amour's book, *Lonesome Gods*, and reconsiders perhaps there is enchantment in such isolation. On the California desert, he puzzles over the complex water control trenches that seem irrelevant in this dry period. Finally they reach Bartholomew, California and drive into Los Angeles. It being evening, they take the first accommodation available.

The next morning, while Gavin goes for an early morning run, Percy rents a room at a motor motel in Huntington Park. It is only a short drive to the pool and track and the price is right.

When they unpack, Gavin asks, "Do you think I'll see anything but the marathon and the cycle races?"

"Ha, ha, ha, I can get any track tickets you want, no sweat, most at cost."

Gibb's confidence baffles Gavin. Could the Canadian newspapers' claim of total sellouts be false? How much would it cost?

Gibb excuses himself a minute, walks down one level to the motel lobby and purchases the Los Angles Times. Back in the room, he starts thumbing through. "Let me check ticket outlets-mm-here's one, not too far, Slauson and Vermont. It's not the most affluent part of L. A. but they just might have what we want. It opens at 10:00 a.m. That gives us thirty minutes. You won't pay any agent's fee here. My tickets purchased in Sudbury were costly with Sears' cut. Let's go over and see."

Gibb wheels the station wagon into a shopping mall beside a McDonald's. With about one hundred people milling about Gibb says, "Looks good Gavin. With this many here there must be tickets for more than fencing." Gibb finds what appears to be the end of the line and unfolds his *Los Angeles Times*.

Gavin studies Percy Gibb sporting his white cap with a red maple leaf, a 1976 Olympic pin on his golf shirt, and a shoulder bag with a kangaroo embossed on it. He reasoned the widowed Mr. Gibb organizes his summer holidays to coincide with international competitions.

The torrid sun, after burning off the last patch of smog, makes direct contact with the mall's black asphalt. Singeing heat suddenly makes Gavin giddy. Running first thing in the morning without breakfast wasn't too smart he concludes. "How about a drink Mr. Gibb?" Gavin asks.

"Iced tea would be great."

"Sure, anything else?"

Gibb shakes his head.

Gavin returns with Gibb's iced tea and an Egg McMuffin for himself.

They watch people as they emerge from the ticket trailer. They either wave tickets ecstatically or grumble at the security officer.

Gavin purchases Gibb's extra tickets for the days Baumann is swimming. At the ticket outlet a beaming Gavin gets what he wants for everything but the last day of track.

Gibb chuckles at Gavin's shock. Gibb knows from experience that unsold tickets from satellite centers are returned to the host city the last few days. "We'll get that final ticket at the stadium. There are always people who can't make it at the last minute."

At dinner Gavin remembers Tanner telling him about a track conference. After verifying the details on a card in his wallet, Gavin says, "Mr. Gibb, I think I'll take in a symposium on distance running in Santa Monica tomorrow."

"Well," Gibb says, scratching his chin, "I wouldn't mind frolicking in those Santa Monica breakers. The swimming finals start late afternoon. I could at least get you there."

In the Sheraton Wiltshire, Gavin hears Peter Coe, father and coach of Olympic 1,500-metre champion Sebastian, expound on his son's training. It looks simple to slowly increase the number of hills run per year in training up to a phenomenal number. But as Mr. Coe points out, it took his son ten years to increase from fifteen to forty runs in a single session up a specific hill. Coe explains how he planned his son's competitions to create the biggest impact on team selectors. This is shocking to Gavin when he considers even an Olympic Champion has to show great concern about making his country's team. Gavin inhales deeply and sighs when Coe divulges the speed of Sebastian's ten-mile winter training runs.

In the afternoon, Gavin sees a film on the life of the great Lassie Viren. The four-time Finnish Olympic Champion trains on identical rural roads to those found around Sudbury. I've got everything I need; it's merely a matter of getting out and doing it, he assures himself.

The Olympic Pool events take place at the University of Southern California, Swimming Center. Gibb glowers with contempt when he finds his seats for Baumann's 400-metre Individual Medley Final. Gibb says to Gavin with a voice everyone from twenty metres around can hear, "Bloody hell,

I bought tickets for swimming not diving." The tickets Gibb so painstakingly purchased in Sudbury, the first day they accepted orders, are at the diving pool—not the swimming pool—and twenty metres behind the swimmers' starting blocks. To even see the swimmers start one has to stand on one's seat and turn ninety degrees. As well, the late afternoon sun is shining directly into their eyes. Gibb puts up with it for the first three races; however, when the starter has Baumann's race on the blocks, he bounds to the top of the stand with Gavin a step behind in the good viewing section. The ushers don't flinch.

As Baumann thrashes his way through the water, Gavin thinks of Arvo's idea on achievement in sport. He shouts himself voiceless trying to bias Arvo's theory.

When Baumann takes undisputed charge, Gibb erupts in high squeaky sounds, "He's putting on a clinic for them." Following Baumann's final touch that stops the running time, tears streak down Gibb's cheeks. He remains speechless for several minutes, while he shakes his head in disbelief. With eyes stretched wide in rapture, he says, "I've witnessed a Canadian swimmer win an Olympic gold." While he hugs Gavin he says, "This is what the Olympics are all about! A lad can come from a remote place and be tops in the World. You don't have to have that big city advantage."

Gavin has goose flesh when Baumann tosses Frisbees to the crowd on his parade to the victory podium. Without a trace of Canadian conservatism "O Canada" reverberates through the summer air. Gavin silently vows to someday climb to the centre of an Olympic podium.

At the track and field competition three days later, Mary Decker, the darling of the Los Angeles crowd, assembles for the 3,000-metre final. Her gold earrings and pendant match her royal status as reigning world champion.

Just as Mary passes Gavin's section of the stadium, a middle-aged lady sitting beside him jumps to her feet. In her exhilaration, she unwittingly whacks Gavin's face with her shoulder purse. Then, with Iroquoian ferocity, shrieks,

"Come on Mary," as though the very survival of the United States was at stake.

Experienced athletes running in a pack adjust to each others' idiosyncrasies effectively when everything is consistent. Zola Budd, Mary's closest rival, by running in bare feet creates a special problem. Some athletes fear fouling Zola and allow her excessive space. This exasperates others. The reactions to Zola start with stilted movements, shift to physical jostling, and end with America's heroine flat on her back in the infield.

Gasps, stunned silence, and then vicious booing erupt. Budd, befuddled, fades from medal contention. Gavin jumps to his feet to cheer Canadian, Lynne Williams, as she picks up the bronze in the mayhem. The appropriateness of the saying, "It's never over 'till it's over," resounds in Gavin's mind.

In the 1,500-metre men's final, Gavin relishes Sebastian Coe's smiling glance as he passes the flagging opposition on the last bend. Here's a man so disgustingly fit he can feast his eyes on his crumbling opponents at the most critical part of an Olympic final. Coe's coy look freezes in Gavin's memory as the epitome of preparation. He vows it isn't sufficient to be as good as his rivals; he has to be that much better. How he can achieve this plagues him the rest of the Games and all the way back to Sudbury.

Chapter 22

In Sudbury, Gavin decides on a total commitment. He makes this decision without contacting his coach who has now moved to Ottawa. Tanner obtained a leave of absence from the university and accepted the job of Technical Coordinator for the Canadian Track and Field Association. Gavin, fearing Tanner's more conservative approach, disregarded his suggestion that they keep in touch weekly.

Two months later during lunch, following a traumatology class, Lisa says to Gavin, "You've survived the first two months of your suicidal training, but how much longer do you think you'll last?"

Gavin shifts his gaze from his ham sandwich to Lisa's intense eyes. With an edge in his voice he says, "This is for keeps, Lisa. After Los Angeles, I know what I have to do, and I'm doing it."

"But you're the one who taught me to do things gradually. Don't you still believe that?"

"To a point yes. I've gone over my quality schedule with Tanner. It's the other stuff I've doubled."

"Does he know?" Lisa asks as she rolls an apple around on the palm of her hand.

"Not exactly. I told him about blending in more hill work. There're no big races coming up. Now is the time to build a base."

Lisa, observing Gavin, calculates the creases around his eyes have lengthened another centimetre in the last month. She adds, "Well I think you're nuts. Your body can't take it."

"We'll see," Gavin says with a touch of disdain and adds, "at least I don't waste half an hour each practice stretching. You could do an extra five kilometres if you cut it to five minutes."

"Okay, let's see who's injury free the longest," Lisa replies.

"Injuries have nothing to do with stretching. My grandmother's flexible and she only walks. If you don't do anything hard, you won't get stiff or risk injury." After saying this Gavin stands, twists his paper bag into a rope and slams it into a garbage bin. Lisa's eyes droop as Gavin mopes off biting his lower lip.

In late November, Tanya, now a resident proctor, has Gavin over for pizza. While she prepares the salad, she intercepts Gavin's eyes stalking her. She controls her dismay at how shrivelled his eye sockets look. While Gavin cuts the pizza, she notices the way his cheekbones jut over taut caverns of skin. When he twists his head, muscles in his neck pop into oblique cords.

After dinner Tanya inserts a family video, taken by her dad at their summer cottage. Within seven minutes Gavin's head slips through Tanya's blond hair, nudges her opal earring, and comes to rest on her shoulder; he is asleep.

"Gavin," Tanya whispers.

Gavin jerks his head up and blinks.

Tanya, with a furrowed brow, says, "You're wearing yourself out—overdoing it!"

"Just a bit tired, Tan—. There was a bright sun this afternoon and it bleached the zip out of me."

"What happened last night when you did the same thing and the sun hadn't been out all day?"

Gavin has steeled himself for such a comment. He feared Tanya's lack of a training commitment would dilute his all-out drive. He jumps to his feet and says, "If that's the way you feel, to hell with it! See you!" Gavin grabs his jacket, struts to the door, squirms into his moccasin-type shoes, and leaves.

Tanya rushes over, her mouth agape. She stares at him as he recedes down the hall; her cheeks twist into a malignant question mark.

If she thinks I'll cut training 'cause I can't stay awake during a boring video, she's loony, Gavin says to himself as he walks to his apartment. For more than an hour, he paces around the newspaper-stacked coffee table, his jacket still in hand. Was he fair? Was he going overboard? Every time he questions himself, the vision of Sebastian Coe rushes through his memory; he knows he can't wish himself into being the best; he has to earn it.

Though tired, he can't sleep. Finally after reading the paperback *The Eye of the Needle*, his eyelids droop.

Next morning, he struggles through a snow squall walking to his motor learning class. Following the lecture, he crawls back into bed rather than do his customary run; he is sleepy and miserable. He wakes in an hour to the sound of thrashing snow against the windowpane. To hell! I can't wait any longer; I have to expect this weather.

He slips into stretch pants he won in a Hamilton road race; covers his sweat top with a nylon shell, and snatches a toque from his improvised clothesline. Three fingers poke through the ends of a cloth glove. It'll do, he decides, as long as I keep my hand clenched. Then he stares at a new pair of flats lying in an open box. He notices the laces aren't threaded; he settles for a well-used laced pair.

On the run, snow-laden wind peppers his face and stings the corneas of his eyes. Gavin regrets, as he charges along, that he is not wearing a peak cap under his toque. At the conservation area he swerves around a closed gate and scurries over a trail bisecting a field of reforested pine.

Five minutes later he tackles a more primitive bush path undulating over roots and rocks and snow-covered gravel. Blocked by dense pines, the strafing wind loses its sting. Not such a bad day after all Gavin figures, and cranks the pace.

Gavin's thoughts of Tanya spark fresh flushes of adrenaline that fuel a series of bursts over the snow-laden sanctuary. He attacks one hill and is descending the next when his right leg slips. Arms flail, but they can't prevent his buttocks from hurtling down on his misaligned leg. He hears a muffled crack as he sprawls on snow-covered ice. When he sits, he sees his foot twisted forty-five degrees out of alignment with his leg, and he can't wiggle his toes. Nerve damage with a fracture he concludes and sighs. It is exactly what Dr. Robinson covered in traumatology class.

With teeth bared and eyes riveted to the fractured leg, he moans, "I'm ruddy well finished as a runner." He closes his eyes in surrender.

Giant snowflakes melt into his stretch pants and provoke volleys of haphazard chilling. This tightens his pectoral muscles like the straps of a strait jacket. Additional gusts magnify the constriction. But he can still move his shoulders. When he reassesses his injury he can again wiggle his toes—no nerve damage. Muscle spasms, he reasons have splinted the injured leg sufficiently to prevent further injury if he moves.

But where can he go? If he turns back it would take three kilometres to get to habitation; if he continues to the beach, the road to the new homes would be one kilometre. The sound of hammering and a faint bark from across nearby Ramsey Lake convinces him to go on.

How could he move? He swallows hard. His arms shake violently against his chest. This time the contractions double in duration. Even if he crawled to a tree for support and climbed to a stand it would be impossible to hop and maintain balance let alone the jarring from each landing to the injured leg. He has to stay close to the ground. From a sitting position, his weight supported by his hands, he can straighten his good bent knee and heave his rump thirty centimeters behind himself. Then, by shifting his hands, he can continue this backwards action like a retreating crawfish.

Within fifteen minutes, cold obliterates any sensitivity in his injured leg. Instead of dragging it in snow to restrain swelling, he lifts it. He also unrolls the nylon hood of his jacket and ties it over his toque.

An hour later and still 600 metres from the beach road, his non-injured leg lacks skin sensitivity but the knee still functions; the backward thrusts continue.

The sigh of relief on reaching the beach changes to horror for the unobstructed wind now rips through him. He must cross the open beach quickly and defy the north wind.

Spasm paralyzes his arms and shoulders; he sits with his head buried in his arms. He tries drawing the knee of his functioning leg to his chest and binding it with his arms to trap his body heat. His muscles relax enough to continue his crablike action. In thirty metres his body again seizes. He hugs himself but it takes longer to get movement. How long can he do this he wonders before the thrashing wind brings him to a halt?

With a glance over his shoulder, he finds he has only 200 metres remaining to the sheltered road. If he stalls out there, surely someone will find him in time. He decides on a last major assault. With partial protection, while he passes behind the changing cabins, he thinks it possible. But the lashing wind pins him to the spot. He slumps to the snow—beaten. Out of curiosity, he twists his neck to see how close he crabbed his way to the road. A mirage of two people approaching spooks him.

He closes his eyes to clear his mind. An object touches his shoulder. Gavin's stark stare starts at the hiker's glove and ends in a surge of elation at the rescuer's face.

With anxious eyes probing him, Gavin explains, "My leg is bro—ken and I'm—v—v—very cold."

The lady runs toward the source of the hammering. The gentleman drapes his coat over Gavin. The carpenter arrives with a truck. Clutching his arms around the necks of his rescuers, Gavin hops on his good leg to the vehicle. In the truck's cab, he shudders all the way to the hospital. Thirty minutes later a nurse tells him his temperature is 34 degrees Celsius. After many hours of waiting and two sessions of x-rays, an ambulance driver takes him to another hospital for surgery. His many requests for something to drink go unheeded. He enters the operating room at nine that evening.

On waking from the anesthetic, Gavin smiles at his straightened leg. After so many hours in a misaligned spasm, his leg muscles feel unnaturally straight.

The next morning Gavin wakes when a blue-coated technician attaches electrodes to his chest. What's this? Did they screw up? His suspicion intensifies when his breakfast consists of only a cup of coffee and a glass of orange juice. The full tray at lunch suppresses his fear of going back under the scalpel.

The orthopedic surgeon visits in the afternoon. Studying charts and looking at Gavin over the bare upper half of his glasses he states, "You fractured your fibula and dislocated your ankle. We sutured ligaments on both sides of the ankle and anchored the joint with a couple of temporary screws."

"Good! Thanks."

After some joking the physician asks, "Do you get short of breath when you run?"

"Oh yeah," Gavin smiles, "after a fast hour run it takes a full three minutes to breathe normally."

With a grin the doctor continues, "Do you get dizzy when you run?"

Gavin, surprised the joke was continuing, replies with an abrupt, "No."

The doctor straightens, removes his glasses and with a solemn voice says, "From the irregular enzymes in your blood, I would suggest a heart attack caused the fall."

"Not a chance!" Gavin replies, but the doctor doesn't listen. He folds and puts his glasses in his vest pocket, checks his wristwatch and leaves.

First thing, the next two mornings Gavin has electrocardiograms taken. On his fourth day the orthopaedic surgeon visits again. He balances his glasses in his left hand while he says in a grave voice, "There are abnormalities in your ECG's which are fluctuating daily."

Gavin smiles.

The surgeon says, "You're taking this difficult news very well."

"Hey," Gavin replies, "it's not difficult news. I know there can't be too much wrong with a pump that can keep a man running sixteen kilometres through a bush trail in an hour. I doubt there's a heart in the city can match it."

The orthopedic surgeon grins, stands straight and says, "I'll have the cardiologist stop in today." He folds his glasses and leaves.

Gavin stares at the snow falling outside with a frown. The anxiously awaited cardiologist doesn't show that day or the next.

When the cardiologist hasn't arrived by the third promised morning Gavin threatens to sign himself out if his orthopedic surgeon doesn't. But the cardiologist does appear.

"I can't detect anything abnormal," the heart specialist concludes after fourteen minutes of probing with his stethoscope, "but arrange for an echocardiogram with my office to make sure."

Gavin's head slumps; his eyes close and the image of Sebastian Coe scooting around in front of everyone flickers through the heavy mist in his mind.

Chapter 23

Frigid air whips Gavin's forehead the moment he hobbles outside. He clamps his crutches under his arms and stretches his hands to lower his toque. With the next gust, he prolongs his inspiration to savour the tingle on his wet lips.

After Lisa pulls over in her Volkswagen, Gavin tosses his crutches and plastic bag with his running gear onto the back seat. He settles himself in front and guides his injured leg in with his hands.

The plastic bag tumbles open when Lisa accelerates onto Ramsey Lake Road. With the musty pervasive odor Gavin says, "I guess my running outfit hasn't had a breath of air since the accident."

Gavin stares out the small clearing in the frosted window and says, "I'm a cracked up hack. It's tough enough making it to the top with everything going for you, now I haven't a chance. All that effort to prove I could do something if I gave it my all—trashed. Now I'm nothing but a one legged steeplechaser—."

Lisa smiles and then feels numb, for the eyes peering from under the ski toque have lost their defiance and that was what she respected most about him. She turns up the heat to melt his frown. Soon beads of perspiration trickle on his forehead.

Gavin smirks at a runner with two bulky sweatsuits lumbering like a bear down Ramsey Lake Road. "Look at that, half those joggers grope around like zombies; they don't push themselves. For them to break a leg would give them an excuse not to train, but for me, I'm ruined. Running keeps me going. It gives me a specific purpose in life. Now I've nothing!"

Lisa creases her forehead and says out of the side of her mouth, "It all depends on how you look at it."

Gavin shifts his plaster cast and replies, "Suppose so, but what's the use if you can't do what excites you?"

"What do you mean? You can start right now on the bike in the lab. Ride with your good leg."

Gavin sighs heavily and chews on the back of his teeth in silence until they arrive back at residence.

Lisa ties off the plastic bag with Gavin's running clothes and carries it in. She waits at the elevator while Gavin picks up a fistful of mail. A stench of fish greets them when the porter unlocks Gavin's door.

Gavin hobbles straight to the divan and elevates his aching leg. Lisa hunts for the odour. A tap drips in the kitchen leaving a clear straight line bisecting a plate's macaroni remnants. Lisa pushes the plates aside but nothing looks responsible for the odor under the avalanche of dishes. Three opened bottles of jam, one carton of honey, and one of peanut butter share the table with breadcrumbs and last week's newspapers. When Lisa looks on top of the refrigerator she utters, *sacrement,* and uses a plastic bag to snare the green, mossy remains of a half-eaten can of sardines. She sidesteps a stack of *Los Angeles Times* Special Olympic Issue newspapers to drop it under the sink. On a coffee table a nest of trophies, including the amethyst crystal penholder she has given him, form anchors for a maze of spider webs. All chairs serve as clotheslines for sweatsuits, T-shirts, and shorts.

Gavin squirms when Lisa heads toward the bathroom with his putrid bag of running clothing. Mr. Clean hasn't touched his bathtub since last summer.

On her return, Lisa spots his Ontario Team sleeping bag from the 1981 Canada Games, half open across his bed. Above his desk she pauses to check a huge graph with the number of kilometres he covers each week plotted in red. She frowns at the precipitous rise in the three weeks preceding his accident.

With Gavin looking comfortable, Lisa says, "Must get to my 11 o'clock, see you."

"Thanks, Lisa." Gavin says, catching her glance before she retreats out the door. He repositions his plaster cast on his living room divan and changes cushions supporting his shoulders. The crutches he has carefully placed against the wall close to him slide to the floor as though having a will of their own. He blushes, when his thoughts drift to his argument with Lisa over stretching, before his mishap. He closes his eyes.

Gavin wakes convinced he should quit school to pump gas. What's the use with a broken leg, an ankle screwed back in place, and the possibility of a damaged heart? He stands on his good leg, works his way behind the divan to pick up his crutches and moves to the window. The isolated snowflakes that shunt around so freely in the wind convince him he can't quit yet.

He makes a strong coffee, clamps the cup handle with his index finger against the crutch handle and delicately swings himself to the bedroom. He grasps his mail and starts to tear open the letters: books overdue, money overdrawn, and university tuition still not paid by the Ontario Athletes' Assistance Fund. Gavin drops the mail on the floor, moans, and falls asleep.

He wakes suddenly thinking of Andy Tanner. Why did Tanner leave the University to work in Ottawa? Does he feel responsible for Scott's deceit? Why did Tanya realize only a fraction of her potential as an athlete? Gavin remembers with sorrow rejecting Tanner's suggestion about keeping in touch weekly.

Sport was worth the sacrifice, he decides, but there are basic things that can't be ignored. He starts by hobbling to the vacuum cleaner closet. By the end of the week he is doing fifteen minutes of cycling with his left leg. He has also borrowed Lisa's notes from the courses they share.

In a couple of weeks a toothy technician vibrates off Gavin's cast. Gavin frowns at the puffy, sutured, white skin on the inside of his ankle. The outside, with two small bulges interspersed along a line of sutures, looks no better. Shreds of peeling skin hang from his shrunken calf. The charge nurse supervises the student nurse removing the stitches. When the student nurse finishes she says, "Aren't you the runner, I mean the former runner?"

"Yes, I'll be racing again someday," Gavin says, in a non too convincing tone. His lip curls in disgust when he palpates his flabby calf.

"This should do you," the technician says when he finishes wrapping a dripping Fiberglas tape around an elastic stocking. It quickly hardens.

While exercising on the cycle ergometre, Gavin starts giving his broken right leg a ride around on the pedal. Soon the injured leg is making a minor and then a moderate contribution to the cycling effort.

Eight weeks later the same grinning technician removes the Fiberglas cast. When Gavin leaves the hospital on crutches, two layers of elastic stocking are all that protect his swollen ankle. Each day he palpates the tender areas around the incisions but finds no change. Gavin moves from cycling with both legs, to walking without crutches, and then to slow running. But his rigid ankle feels like a clubfoot.

Using a mild anesthetic, the orthopedic surgeon probes into the bulges and removes two screws. After a couple of days of non-weight bearing activity, Gavin completes a short run with a much fuller range of motion. Now that he has the equipment, can he make that team Tanner mentioned last September that was going to Greece in August?

Chapter 24

On Sudbury streets, the mid-March sun brings out smiles on many a shopper's face. In the fields, the melting snow gives birth to gurgling creeks. On the roads, runners stash toques and gloves to more intimately welcome the sun.

Amongst the sun's greeters, Gavin has the broadest smile, for the azure sky reminds him of a Greek post card enclosed in Tanner's last letter. His coach's communication has details of the Athens August competition and Canada is committed to all events. Gavin decides with an ankle limiting him to four kilometres of running a day, there is no rush to renew his passport.

That evening, however, he formulates a strategy to increase his odds. He tries loading mainly his good left leg by means of a non-running activity. He settles for step-ups on a wooden bench. Each evening he musters whatever energy he has in raising and lowering his body weight, having his left leg do the lifting. His bouts are set for an exertion time of eight minutes that approximates his competitive steeplechase time. A week later, he is on his third session of eight minutes of stepping, when Tanya approaches his door to return his motor learning assignment. With her fist poised to knock, she hears rhythmical noises and much huffing with long sighs. My God! Who's visiting him? She lowers her arm with a demure smile.

Gavin, in squeezing out the last bit of zip from a disjointed body, lacks initiative in cultivating new acquaintances. He also fears his athletic vow will collapse if he once more takes in the Thursday night pubs. Instead he tags along with Lisa. Every morning she runs, no matter the weather. She enjoys Gavin's company for her first run each day and, at this point in his rehabilitation, his speed.

But for Lisa her passions mushroom in several directions. Verbal answers to questions she poses in class seldom satisfy her; she makes a point of chasing down details in the library. Occasionally, she submits her opinions in the Francophone student newspaper *L'Orignal*.

Lisa, after deciding to take in a movie, stops to see if Gavin is interested. Not having been to his apartment since the accident, she says on entering, "What's this, have you had the cleaning lady in?" She rushes over the spotless rug, through the newspaper-free floor and checks the kitchen. She gives a proud parent-like sigh saying, "Well."

Lisa's reaction warms Gavin. He's getting back his old drive and has someone who takes his dedication as normal. They become closer friends and occasionally lovers, but Cupid's arrow never unites their individual pathways.

In the second week of April, while Gavin is strolling back from his final exercise physiology exam, he spots Mr. Thoburn in his Audi on campus.

Thoburn recognizes Gavin and pulls over, "Great to see you Gavin! Sorry to learn of your accident." When he sees Gavin's face light up he adds, "You managing?"

"It used to ache, but I get away with more now."

"I think Tanya's lost without her running," Thoburn says.

"Yeah, it's a tough activity if you expect too much from it. A lot of things happen that don't appear fair. On the other hand, I guess I need ups and downs to keep my life exciting."

"You and Tanya seeing each other?"

"We travel in different circles. Can't handle her social pace." When Thoburn's eyes sink to his ignition key, Gavin says, "Don't worry about Tanya. I hear she's running the Student Association. Evidently she's taken over from the clown who was president."

"I guess you're right. She always had a flair for doing things. Well, take care now." Thoburn says, when he notices a car patiently waiting behind him.

After Mr. Thoburn rings Tanya's room, she bounds down the stairs. They drive to Casey's Restaurant. Over a Caesar salad Thoburn says, "I'm trying to interest a biologist at Science North into using some of my takes on fox life. I staked out a den near the cottage. Incidentally the old place is quite comfortable with the new foundation and revamped water system to the lake." Thoburn pauses and studies the hint of puffiness around Tanya's eyes. "And how've you been?"

"Okay, I guess. In a couple weeks I'll be out of here. I've had enough."

"Sorry to hear that Tanya. I'm fascinated by the changes I've experienced with regular activity." Thoburn hesitates, seeing Tanya's long face, and stretches for a sip of tea.

Tanya stares intently at her chili.

After a minute of silence Thoburn continues, "Been taking clips of the city's amateur sports action for CRZ Television one weekend in four. I stay in Toronto a few days while I'm down, but I'm always anxious to head north."

"How's the rehabilitation going?"

"Exercising has lowered my blood pressure and changed that stuff in my blood that carries cholesterol. In other words, I pay as I go— have you any plans for next year?"

"I applied at a couple of places for a Master's program but didn't follow up with references. School's a drag. The weekend track trips in earlier years gave me a break. I wish I hadn't given it up." A sly smile slides across Tanya's face, one Mr. Thoburn hasn't seen since she misbehaved as a child. Thoburn grips her hand then hugs her. Her warm response makes him feel she has resolved her nonsense over his retirement.

Back at residence before leaving Thoburn says, "Keep trucking kid, exams will soon be over."

In May, Gavin no longer needs the elastic stocking and enters all-comers competitions. He learns from Tanner that if he finishes within 10 seconds of his best '84 performance he could gain selection.

Gavin again sings in the shower after running. His leg responds superbly. He is able to run almost as fast but never as long as he could before the accident. Everything is honed to a fine edge by the trials in Ottawa.

But he finishes well behind the new national champion, Brian Cotter, in the 3,000-metre steeplechase. What more could I expect, Gavin asks himself as he pokes an arm into his sweat jacket after the race. His fight back to fitness, although successful in one sense, leaves him deflated in another. Finally he decides he has come a long way.

Following a post competition reception, Tanner leaves for the team selection meeting, while Gavin returns to the Chimo Hotel. At three in the morning a buzz arouses Gavin. Pressing the receiver to his ear he hears, "You're on the team; we leave next Sunday; I've got to get back to the meeting, details later. Bye."

Gavin shakes his head a couple of times but the receiver was in his hand and that was undeniably Tanner's voice. He jumps to his feet and prances around clenching and relaxing his fists.

Tanner didn't mention it took his intervention in the meeting to get Gavin on the team. Tanner, as distance coach for the trip to Greece, explained Gavin's injury and the extent of his recovery. The selection committee reconsidered Gavin after a javelin thrower withdrew with serious tendonitis. Over the Atlantic, Tanner winces when he watches Gavin limp to the washroom. He wonders how long it will be before he is charged with favouritism.

The Canadian Team transfers onto British Airways at Heathrow and continues to Athens. They are happy to leave England for the constant loudspeaker warnings advising against touching abandoned articles makes them feel in a war zone.

The sun is sinking into a copper sky when Gavin follows Tanner into the Athens' Airport. It is a warm arid evening. A member of the welcoming committee greets them at the baggage carousel. Tanner introduces himself to the middle-aged Greek hostess who speaks Americanized English. She welcomes the athletes as though they were all in her circle of friends.

Rotating blue lights on the police escort guide the Canadian bus to the President Hotel. While waiting for his luggage Gavin scans the distant mountains. His chest pounds when he realizes the people of this country organized the first Modern Olympic Games.

Chapter 25

"Yes, we need three more rooms than we reserved," Canadian Team Manager Bert Sandstrom insists. A lady on the reception desk picks up the telephone.

A gentleman, wearing a sky blue jacket with grey flannels, strides across the lobby from the competition desk; his lips twitch on a cigarette. His administrative assistant's high heels reverberate behind him. The gentleman opens his file and studies several lists. When the quick-stepping assistant reaches him, she points to the stack of lists and shakes her head. The gentleman removes his cigarette and paws the air in her direction. She backs off with a forced smile, tugs at her waist jacket, and frowns because Sandstrom receives three additional keys.

Sandstrom nods, smiles, and says, "Sorry for the extra trouble," while he gives them each a pin with a maple leaf, the assistant forces a smile.

With his room key in hand, Gavin carries his luggage across the marbled floor to the diminutive elevators. When he sees the throng of athletes ahead of him anxiously peering at the slow-moving floor indicator, he chucks his luggage against a nearby wall and sits. Pole-vaulter Jake, his roommate, drops his bags also, and returns to the lobby to supervise the storage of his three poles.

Although it is close to midnight, footsteps echo with the five o'clock excitement of Times Square. A coach, recognizing a friend, motions with his head toward a table in a bar a half-story above where Gavin is sitting. His friend bursts forth with a smile and follows. Within minutes other coaches join the banter at a table above Gavin's lounge chair.

They speak French, and Gavin recognizes the names of his three top rivals, Korir, Hackney, and Koech. Though the steeplechase is not scheduled for five days, hearing these names makes Gavin's liver quiver. He takes several deep diaphragmatic breaths but it doesn't relax him. The recent performances tossed into the discussion are much better than his. Fifteen minutes later Jake is back and the elevator free.

At the seventeenth floor hallway, Gavin muffles a cough. He pauses to scan the chain-smoking security guard seated close by whose eyes never leave his crossword while Gavin fumbles with his keys. Jake darts into the room, drops his bags on a bed, and rushes to the bathroom.

Gavin immediately heads for the balcony. A fresh breeze strikes his face when he opens the sliding door. At a distance, strings of road lamps, resembling lights on a Christmas tree, wind up a hillside. Seventeen stories below, screeching tires, revving motors, and incessant horns, rupture Gavin's meditation. Did Aristotle and Plato gaze at these same hills? He creeps closer to the steel balustrade and looks over, but resists leaning against it for fear the builders' passion for ouzo carried into their working day. Cautiously he surveys the front of the hotel. At the main entrance, match-stick figures strut like Charlie Chaplin. An armoured vehicle, complete with machine gun turret, is parked in readiness around the corner. At this height it reminds Gavin of a child's toy. A fire ladder truck stays poised behind it. The Ancient Greeks declared an armistice during their celebratory Games; the present Greeks aren't as trusting.

Gavin's mind drifts to the striking achievements the Greeks made to civilization and wonders how these undistinguished-looking Greeks could have such a rich heritage? What is it that changes the thinking and the energy levels of a nation? There must be some remnants of the original gene pool. Gavin scours his mind for reasons a person or nation's vitality changes.

"Your turn," Jake says, "but take a bath, that shower head never stays put when you open the faucet." Jake, towelling himself, walks out on the balcony. He then returns to finish drying his blond muscular body in front of the mirror.

In the bath, Gavin runs his fingers over the faded, purple scars at his ankle. The puffiness makes him frown; he shakes his head thinking he should have elevated his leg more during the flight. Raising the injured foot to the tub's edge, he strokes the injury in the direction of his heart, as the therapist suggested.

A few minutes later Jake answers a knock on the door.

"You okay?" Bert Sandstrom asks. With Jake's nod Sandstrom continues: "Breakfast 7:00 to 8:30; buses for training leave at 9:30."

"Thanks," Jake replies and the team manager continues his rounds.

"Glad the training's early, gives me a chance to take pictures of the Parthenon in the afternoon," Jake says as Gavin hangs up his towel.

"I may join you after practice if everything goes well," Gavin says.

At breakfast next day, Tanner loops Gavin's accreditation around his neck and says, "Wear this at all times, and you won't get into trouble."

Starting at 9:20, a.m., athlete after athlete boards the idling bus in front of the hotel. Seven policemen jest on the sidewalk next to the bus; they pause periodically to appreciate the feline contours of the double x chromosomes boarding.

At 9:40 a.m. the gentleman with the sky blue jacket stomps a freshly-lit cigarette on the sidewalk and climbs aboard. Drops of perspiration smear his lists of countries before he nods to the driver to close the door. The driver revs the motor, checks his mirrors, and lunges behind the flashing blue light of a police escort.

Tanner, having competed in Athens several years earlier, stands up. He wants to say that the stadium is in the opposite direction. But the driver pulls to the extreme right at the first intersection and swings into a "U" turn in the busiest juncture in Athens. Police white gloves flash feverishly as the driver achieves his task with a snappy hand-over-hand action on the wheel.

The stadium lights stretch like tall wind-blown palm trees above the immense, yet compact, 68,000 seat structure. The bus follows a lane, through gnarled olive trees, to the rear of the stadium. The driver parks beside three eight lane, tartan training tracks outside the main stadium.

When everyone gapes at the facilities, Tanner says with a chuckle, "You can see these people keep their priorities straight. There are as many polyurethane tracks on this site as there are in all of Ontario."

Gavin ran on the short cropped grass savouring the sun and the feel of the land of the ancient Greeks. He dragged a steeplechase barrier into the infield and did a few bar clearances until he felt limber. The leg he broke had peculiar aches but he was sure it would be okay.

Gavin replaces his T-shirt and reclines on the grass. While he stretches in a hurdling position, a female athlete with a hammer and sickle on her vest comes toward him. She suddenly stops, bends down and opens a shoulder bag next to his. Her flushed, dainty face, her skintight shorts, and the proximity of her curvaceous body all make his heart rate soar. His eyes, like a starving man's surveying a tasty morsel, follow her every move. While stretching overhead into a white T-shirt, tufts of dark reddish-brown hair sprout from each armpit. Gavin's heart stalls. He swallows hard, suppresses a strange smile, and continues with his stretching. Puzzled, he asks himself could his reaction to female beauty be this socially conditioned?

At the shuttle bus rendezvous, Gavin notices a platoon of policemen chatting under a scrubby olive tree. It is easy to visualize the bulldog-looking Socrates, sitting by the hour in this climate, prodding arrogant youth to refine their logic. Gavin considers competing in the nude, as the ancient Greeks' did, would pose no hardship in this climate. Gavin again extends himself on the dry grass and rests his head on his bag. He conjectures how many athletes before him forced their limbs to the brink of collapse on the sacred soil of Greece.

When Tanner squats beside him, Gavin sits up and asks, "Why would they build three warmup tracks on one location?"

Tanner rubs his chin, removes his sunglasses, and surveys the sparsely used tracks, "They wanted to emphasize their leadership in the Olympic movement and to offer a site for the Centennial of the modern Olympic Games in '96."

"Isn't Toronto applying? Wasn't that the reason for building the Sky Dome?"

Tanner nods without enthusiasm. Gavin settles his head back on his bag until the revving of a shuttle bus startles him back into action. When he notices Jake struggling to load his poles, Gavin rises and feeds Jake his poles through the driver's side window. Jake never relaxes unless his poles are close to him.

At lunch Jake asks Gavin, "Are you okay visiting the Acropolis this afternoon? If we go today, we'll recover from any stiffness the standing might cause before the competition."

Gavin thinks a moment and says, "Sure, but I won't stay long; I'm just getting over an injury."

"No, no, just two to three hours will be plenty. I hear taxis are inexpensive."

At three o'clock they wind their way up the long stone steps to the Acropolis. Their white maple leaf embroidered caps offer protection from the fierce Athenian sun. They flash athletic accreditation for free admission and climb and climb, with hundreds of other tourists, the stone steps.

Jake, a University of Toronto history major, thumbs through a booklet he brought with him. First they seek shelter from the intense outside glare by sauntering about in the Acropolis Museum.

Here they eavesdrop on a guide with an America tour who says, "As you can see from the beautiful bodies here depicted, the Greeks were most emphatic in their emphasis on physical prowess; nudity meant nothing to them. The Ancient Greeks believed in the simple perfection of life and strove ceaselessly for that attainment."

When they leave the Museum, Jake moves across to the edge of the cliff to photograph the ruins of an outdoor theatre below the escarpment. Gavin studies the overall architecture and tries to imagine the original colours.

While Jake is studying the rows of semi-circular stone benches, he hears a voice behind him say, "Excuse me, but are you a Canadian student?"

"Eh, yeah, I'm Canadian," Jake replies, turning to face the person speaking.

"How do you do? My name is Leonidas; I welcome you to my country. I have a cousin planning to immigrate to Toronto. I would very much like to talk with you about your country."

Gavin, some distance away, tunes in to another guide who is addressing a group from Brazil in French and is pointing toward the pillars.

A few minutes later Jake rejoins Gavin and says, "Leonidas has invited me to his home for dinner; he wants to learn more about Canada; he also said he has a sister studying Canadian History at university. You don't mind going back on your own?"

"What? Wait a minute. Okay, I know my way back. I'll grab a cab," Gavin says flatly.

"Be back around midnight. It depends on how things go," Jake replies, his blue eyes twinkling.

"Sure," Gavin says with a prolonged expiration. He watches Jake return to the gentleman who initially spoke to him, and he notices two others join them.

Jake scurries off with the three people, never turning back to notice Gavin's anxiety.

Jake doesn't return at midnight, nor is he back next morning. At breakfast, Gavin talks to Jake's coach.

"That ass! By the time a guy reaches university, you'd think he'd have some sense!"

When Jake doesn't show by noon, the jump's coach tells the team manager. The Chef-de-Mission contacts the Canadian Embassy.

Gavin is uneasy at practice; his timing over the steeplechase water jump is terrible. He hasn't told Tanner about Jake.

Tanner, shocked by Gavin's clumsiness, makes light of it. He knows any concern on his part will magnify Gavin's distress.

At five in the afternoon the police locate a narcotized person fitting Jake's description in a run-down *taverna*. "This isn't the first time this has happened," the Canadian diplomat says to the team manager. "We've had quite a few of our people taken advantage of through feigned hospitality."

After a thorough medical examination at the hospital, Jake is sufficiently alert to join the team manager who takes him back to the hotel by cab. Jake mumbles as they undress him and cover him with a sheet. It is not clear if Jake recognizes anyone. Gavin sits on the easy chair watching a perspiring Jake. A stale odour surrounds him. Jake contorts his face and moans; his breathing gets deeper and rhythmical as he goes back to sleep. An hour later, the Greek physician who attended Jake earlier stops by. The doctor shakes his head intermittently while he fills out a lengthy report.

The organizers, no doubt hoping to maintain a high profile for staging first-rate athletic competitions, keep Jake's misadventure from the media.

At the team meeting the next day, team manager Sandstrom circulates invitations to a reception at the Canadian Embassy. He gives each group of four a map of the embassy's location and says, "Have each taxi fill out some kind of receipt. I'll reimburse you."

With Jake awake but not talking, the jump's coach stays with him while the rest make their way to the reception. The maps copied from the Canadian Embassy are naturally in English and almost unintelligible to the taxi drivers.

At the Embassy, Tanner drifts to a seat with a Greek beer. As he watches athletes doing stunts off the one-metre diving board, he hears someone behind him say, "How's your crippled steeplechaser making out? I hope his swimming is better than his water jumping."

Andy Tanner turns to see Raymond Dubois, the sprint coach.

Tanner ignores the remark, but the corners of his lips droop. Dubois immediately prattles, "Ha, ha, ha, all the way to Greece for experience."

"Pipe down," the head-of-delegation says to Dubois. Raymond Dubois coaches at the same track club in Montreal as Brian Cotter. Dubois' best friend in Montreal is Brian Cotter's steeplechase coach. This same friend was runner-up to Andy Tanner for the Ottawa position with Canadian Track and Field.

When Gavin returns to the hotel, a Greek detective is waiting for him.

Chapter 26

A squat man pops a cigarette under his bushy mustache and lights it. He nods toward the lobby chairs. The seeping smoke from his nostrils makes him squint. Through a female translator he asks, "What did this guy look like?"

Gavin states what he remembers and watches the translator contort her face on listening and relax as the words flow in translation. They continue through the translator.

"Was he alone?" the detective asks and takes a long slow drag.

"I thought so, but when Jake decided to go with him I noticed a couple of other guys join. It gave me a creepy feeling."

"Could you describe these people?"

"Nothing special—they didn't act like tourists; they knew, without hesitation, where the nearest exit was when Jake agreed to join them."

"Anything else you can think of?"

"No—only that Jake was supposed to have dinner at this guy's home."

The detective hands Gavin his card and asks, "Call if you remember anything more."

Back in the room Gavin tries to avert staring at red splotches on Jake's face. When he sees Jake's eyes open, he asks, "How you feeling?"

"Okay," but then Jake immediately turns his back on Gavin.

Gavin takes a shower. Seeing Jake in the same position, he asks, "Can I bring you something for lunch?"

"No thanks. I'll go down when it's not so crowded."

"Fine, see you." Gavin returns to the elevator through the smoke-filled hall.

On the elevator he meets the jumps coach who asks, "Is he talking to you? He didn't say a word to me in five hours."

"Not much."

"Too bad, I couldn't get him to look at me. I guess he went through a raw experience. Not much chance he'll be ready for the preliminaries on Friday," the jump's coach says. Next afternoon, Gavin steps out of the hotel in search of a kiosk for post cards. The blazing sun chases him back under cover before he has walked a hundred metres. Returning to his room, he places a chair on the shaded half of the balcony and gazes at the hills.

This sight reminds him of his paperback by Robert Graves on *The Greek Myths*. He retrieves it from his suitcase, opens it, studies the bookmark from a Heathrow shop and starts reading. A knock on the door retracts his heavy eyelids while pursuing the book's introduction.

Tanner enters and says, "I've checked the start lists for the steeplechase. After the top five the talent's sparse." He traces his finger across the top entries in the program. Gavin notices that both he and Brian Cotter are unranked.

"Suits me that they don't have my last year's best time; I always run better as an underdog."

Tanner places a chair beside Gavin and they go over the probable pace for each lap. They then set down tentative tactics.

After avoiding people all week, Jake surprises all by attending the pole vault qualifying rounds. He successfully makes the final. Jake insists on using only a male translator when he confides his experiences to the chain-smoking detective.

On race day the temperature is well over 30 degrees Centigrade. Gavin, on the seventeenth floor balcony, feels an occasional breeze when he continues to read Grave's book. He pauses to stare at the hills and wonders what part mountains played in segregating peoples so they could naturally develop their individuality? Did his time in the bush foster his need to excel as a steeplechase runner? When a sudden ambulance siren jars him out of his reflections, he questions how far civilization has progressed when so many people tolerate so much city clamour. It seems most irreverent in Athens. He checks his watch and decides it's time to leave for the stadium.

The Canadian steeplechasers arrive with coach Andy Tanner one and one-half hours before their race. Easy running occupies the first twenty minutes. Although they don't exchange words, being together provides mutual support in an unfamiliar environment. Later, they separate to do specific warmup drills over hurdles. Gavin concentrates on suppressing the pressure mounting on his eleventh hour selection to the team. Brian Cotter, after beating Gavin handily in the trials, has publicly denounced Gavin's selection to the team. At this moment, Brian Cotter is obsessed with finishing in front of Gavin.

Tanner keeps the athletes under surveillance while they warm up. He knows competing athletes are quick to panic under the slightest provocation. Eventually, Tanner gives them the signal to report.

In the tunnel leading to the stadium infield, Gavin has visions of being in ancient Rome where ferocious lions savoured their essential amino acids at humans' expense. He smiles in a cunning way for this afternoon he plans on doing the clawing.

When they reach track level in the stadium, the sight of officials gorging themselves on free cola makes his stomach jumpy. He checks the washroom entrance for he might suddenly have to vomit. His typical pre-race quiver has invaded his whole body, and he is perspiring. With the ten-minute signal, Gavin finds a quiet corner to rehearse his expected lap times.

After leaving the athletes at the control gate, Tanner climbs to the upper deck to join the Canadian coaches. The moment he claims a vacant seat, Dubois points to a male Greek in a ceremonial skirt on the infield and says, "Look at that—the epitome of Greek manhood." Noticing Tanner sitting directly behind him, he taps Tanner's knee and says, "Why don't you get one of those dresses for your steeplechaser."

As the starter calls the athletes to their marks, Gavin perceives himself being part of the ancient legends. Three laps go by comfortably, so Gavin moves up to the fifth runner's shoulder.

Brian Cotter, however, has found the pace challenging from the start and loses his concentration. The positions remain unchanged for three more laps.

Tanner, in the stands, is recording the lap times of both Canadian athletes. When Gavin moves up, Tanner hears Dubois ask, "Can I get anyone an expresso?"

At the bell, signaling one lap to go, the leading two spurt to a ten-metre advantage. This stuns the three athletes directly in front of Gavin. Gavin burst by them opening a five-metre gap that he maintains. A time of 8:31 is Gavin's best ever.

With Dubois' comments still tickling him, Tanner winds his way to the warmup area to find Gavin. They exchange the same joy a heavyweight boxer and trainer must share when a fighter wins after taking a nine count.

"Dinner's on me in the Plaka," Tanner says, "but get in a twenty minute warmdown on the grass before we head back."

Later that evening they find a *taverna* on Lissikratous Street and order barbecued lamb. The open-air restaurant has an atmosphere of heavy spices, and while they dine throbbing music from a bouzouki trills the air.

When Gavin sips his ouzo, he looks up the street where electric lights glorify the Acropolis. He's sure the spirit of the Greek gods will never leave him.

Next morning, when Gavin shifts his weight on his previously injured leg, searing pain strikes. With a few more steps the pain recedes as strangely as it appeared. He gets on with his packing.

At the airport, Gavin asks to join Tanner to review next year's training. Over wine Tanner says, "Your time here will get you carded by Sports Canada, that means $450 a month; it should help keep you organized."

They dine on lamb shish kebabs. With the removal of the trays, Tanner takes out his notebook and is ready to discuss the training plans for next season's Commonwealth Games. One glance at Gavin and Tanner reaches for his Paris Edition of the *New York Times*. Gavin's chin has sunk to his chest.

Chapter 27

In North Bay, Gavin hands the taxi driver a twenty. He slings the strap of his red Canadian team bag over his shoulder and grips the two smaller pieces. He crosses the street to *grand'mère's*. The papergirl stops and puzzles over his strangely tagged luggage. As Gavin climbs the steps of the front porch, *grand'mère* grins at him from her new gliding chair. A blue veined hand clutches the newspaper; a book balances on her lap. It takes Gavin a moment to realize her large, black bookmark is the handle of a magnifying glass.

"Ah T'cun ça va?" she says.

Gavin embraces her with a kiss on each cheek and says, "You've quite a tan, what have you been doing?"

"I've been straightening tomato plants and other back yard puttering." She leads Gavin to the kitchen and pours him a tall glass of apple juice. Turning to Gavin with a child's excitement, she says, "They tell me you raced in Europe. Athens, wasn't it? Teresa saw it in the *North Bay Nugget*."

"Yes, I sent you a post card. I finished third in a steeplechase. It's a race of less than two miles with barriers three-feet high to get over every so often—what an upside down country Greece is."

"Now let me note what you did." She picks up the pencil tied with string to the hook of a kitchen calendar and jots a few notes. "In Greece you came third, well that's wonderful; I wish I could have managed a visit to Greece."

"It wasn't the Athens I expected *Grand'mère*. People sleep in the day and raise hell at night; most men chain-smoke. That temple, known as the Parthenon, on the other hand, stumped me trying to figure out how they moved all that sculpted marble without modern equipment."

Gavin takes a sip, licks his lips and says, "By the way, tell Uncle Jacques if he still needs another person at Thanksgiving

I'd be happy to join him hunting. Before I left for Athens, he called and said he drew a bull tag."

"All right I'll mention it next Sunday dinner."

"Also would you know where my dad's books are on flying? I've decided to go for a pilot's license."

"Gavin! You be careful," *grand'mère* stares at Gavin for a few moments, her face drawn. She sighs and says, "They're in the front attic in a wooden butter box behind the hanging bearskin sealing off that part we don't heat."

"Merci, Grand'mère."

Gavin spends four days peeling blanched tomatoes, getting trounced in Scrabble, and browsing through his dad's air navigation books. He then returns to the university.

The bustle of students moving in keeps a constant flow of trolleys screeching past his door. Bursts of laughter break out as lost parents seek their children's new quarters. Gavin opens his door and reflects on his reactions when he moved in. He marvels at his passion for hurdling obstacles on the dead run and the manner by which it has changed his life. He smiles at the overloaded trolleys passing in the hallway and secretly hopes the new students will also find their niche at the university. Seeing a mother insist her son keep a vacuum cleaner she has carried to his room—still laden with a price tag—spurs Gavin to reach in his own closet.

His cleaner barely hits full speed before Lisa bursts in saying, "Gavin that was something. You're clicking again. Congratulations!" She kisses him and gives him a series of hugs.

Gavin is fascinated with Lisa's exhilaration. He has not seen her since graduation.

"Yes, Lisa, it came together. It was as though being a runner was the thing to do; the people understood. When I thought back on the ancient Olympics it all made sense—Tanner mentioned you're on your way to Western?"

"I changed my mind about teaching; I couldn't refuse Western's scholarship offer. They have more road races down there as well." Lisa then explores Gavin's living room. It kindles memories of that day she brought him back from the hospital after he had broken his leg. His willingness to ignore so many basic things to pursue something special fascinated her.

Gavin notices while Lisa surveys the rest of his apartment that her new glasses don't slip down her nose. The gold bracelet of alternating *x's* and *o's* circling her wrist glistens when she moves. She is wearing a sea green, tie-dyed top with a scalloped neck and denim mini skirt.

There is a knock on the half-open door; Tanya appears in an old Coast Guard T-shirt and blue jeans.

"Well, how's the world traveller? Congratulations! I was so happy for you." She slaps Gavin's shoulder and embraces him. Tanya breaks off when she notices Lisa return from her inspection.

"Hi Lisa," she says. "Coming back this year?"

"No, off to Western."

"Good for you. Shouldn't be too tough, you being on the Dean's Honour Roll."

"I should be able to handle it. And what have you been up to this summer?"

"Coast Guard on Georgian Bay."

"Fun?"

"Great, except you're stuck for two weeks in an isolated spot—must be off. Good luck in London Lisa; See you Gavin."

"Hey, let me make some coffee?"

"No thanks, my laundry must be dry now." Tanya skips out.

Gavin turns to Lisa, pauses for several seconds and says, "I'm going to miss you, Lisa. You saved me when everything went sour. It won't be the same."

Lisa blushes and puts her arms around Gavin's neck. "Thanks that makes me feel good. I hope I can keep running without you around."

Gavin presses his lips to her cheek; his fingers make small circles on the muscles of her back; she sighs and glances up at him.

When Gavin searches her sticky brown eyes, fresh impulses zip back and forth through his spinal cord; he latches the door.

One hour later, they start a relaxed run over the 10-kilometre Simic trail. It circles beaver ponds and parts of two lakes. This trail is Gavin's favourite when he doesn't want a high quality session. Toward the end of the run, Lisa stumbles on a protruding root. "I won't miss this obstacle course," she groans.

Her words hover in Gavin's mind for he thought she enjoyed the occasional bush whacking as much as he did. Has she forgotten what she grew up on?

As they finish their grilled cheese and tomato sandwiches, Lisa says, "You're not a bad cook. Better get going or I'll hit Toronto traffic." She gathers her damp running gear and squeezess a plastic lid over a steaming cup of coffee. Gavin accompanies her to the parking lot.

"We'll keep in touch," Gavin says. He nudges her shoulder. She clamps sunglasses over her regular eyeglasses, smiles and drives off. Somehow, Gavin suspects running will never command the same priority in her life again.

With his Bachelor's Degree completed and having achieved satisfactory scores on the G-MAT aptitude tests for Business Administration, Gavin is accepted in the Master's program at Laurentian. Money he earns as a residence night clerk goes into flying lessons. If all goes well, he expects to be a licensed pilot by the time he finishes school.

For the month of September Gavin limits his training to a daily one-hour hard run. He, however, initiates three fifteen-minute sessions per week on the permanently setup trampoline used by divers in the swimming pool. The idea of trampolining came from Jake who suggested it was fun and helped develop a spatial sense valuable in vaulting.

Gavin interrupts his training a couple of days to accompany Jacques on a weekend of hunt camp preparation. They arrive at the special patch of lily pads three rapids and ten kilometres down river from the boat launch. They hike in carrying such bulky items as a roll of plastic, cans of camp fuel and a new stovepipe elbow.

The stove, though more rusted, is still serviceable. Upkeep includes firming up the interior horizontal stovepipes held in place with coathanger wire. Behind the camp, they rebuild a tripod to support the new chimney's elbow. Gavin culls three spruce trees to bolster the roof props. As Gavin unrolls plastic, Jacques staples the overlapping sheets to the carpet-covered sides of the roof perimeter poles. A bear's visit requires replacement of the south wall. Finally, that day, Jacques bags the shredded plastic from the reconstruction, while Gavin stacks dry firewood inside. The smell of spruce reminds Gavin of the happy times he had preparing the seven, fly-in camps his dad operated.

That evening, between puffs on his pipe, Jacques says, "That's good Gavin, we've enough wood. Tomorrow we see what's going on in the bush. With a bull tag this year it could be interesting."

Next morning they check Jacques' elevated hides. The first is a triangular shaped platform five metres above ground. It overlooks a long open marsh. It is constructed with two horizontal spruce poles secured at one end to the sides of the same tree and each joined at the opposite end to individual trees one metre apart. Smaller horizontal struts attached to the longer pieces form the basis for the floor. Two side spruce railings, one-half metre and one metre above the floor on each side, act as protective barriers from movement on the elevated platform. They also could serve as a rifle rest. Climbing struts reach up from the ground to the hide's floor.

At the second hide there are fresh bull-moose droppings consisting of cubes of about 3-4 centimetres. On their return to camp, Jacques says, "Look at this," pointing to some newly scarred aspen bark, two metres above the ground. "And 'ere too," as he studies how recently the aspen tops had been bent and chewed off. They spend the rest of the day cutting and clearing deadfall from the trails.

"S.T." Jacques says in Gavin's ear on the way up river before sunset. "In spite of some signs the damn moose might be scarce again this year. I may have to go back to River Valley where I 'unted as a kid even though the tags are more scarce there."

"Jacques, some of those tracks aren't that old. Remember it rained last week."

"Not good, not good dammit. They're just not enough. I don't think that system the Ministry has works, even though they say the 'erd has increased." Jacques keeps the motor in a straight line with his elbow, while he pulls out a pipe. He opens his tobacco pouch between his knees and packs his bowl with his index finger. Jacques sinks under the collar of his orange Mustang jacket and spins his lighter. A cloud of smoke covers his grey beard for a moment, but the pipe doesn't stay lit.

Back in Sudbury Jacques says, "Well Gavin, next Friday at noon, you'll be ready?"

"Sure thing, Jacques."

"Bill Turnbull will join us too."

"Good, see you."

Next week during every run and every session on the trampoline, Gavin wonders about how fresh those tracks actually were. He even gets out his moose-calling tape and practises seductive calls.

Friday afternoon, under a sky of fog and near-zero temperature, three adventurers go north. At the landing, the hood of the truck resonates with the twang of rain. They quickly load the motorboat and cargo canoe.

Five kilometres down river, Gavin reattaches the plastic over the packs in the bow. He tightens the notch on the top of his slicker and straightens his knees to check the penetrating dampness. The twenty-minute hike from the boat warms Gavin for the first time since leaving the truck.

"Thank God we got things ready last week Gavin, or it would 'ave been the shits," Jacques says as they unload their packs in camp. It doesn't take long to get the dry spruce burning and Jacques' old kettle whistling.

Bill Turnbull, Jacques' neighbour from Sturgeon Falls, dumps beef stew from a plastic container into the camp's iron frying pan. Jacques removes stray stands of cobwebs from a saucepan with a paper towel and empties a preserve bottle of *grand'mère's* pea soup. Gavin pulls out some fresh Golden Grain Bread. Sitting on split log benches, they relax over their hot meal. As the sizzling stove chases the humidity out of the air, they plan the next day's hunt.

Jacques and Bill choose the two closest hides: one a kilometre south, the other north a half kilometre on the side of a mountain. Gavin is happy to take the hide on the trail off the end of the lake. He remembers all too clearly his adventure with a cow moose. Those were the days before the Ministry had draws for adult tags.

After dinner, Jacques opens the stove door, removes a flaming twig, and lights his pipe. On returning the stick the flames shoot back at him. "S.T. that's 'ot!" He shakes his fingers a few times. "This 'eat makes me tired, I'm going to turn in after my smoke. I'll set the alarm for six, it'll give us time for something to eat before we 'unt."

Next morning after breakfast, fog covers the lake when Gavin shoves aside the makeshift, plastic, door flap. By the time he puts a touch of skunk scent on his boots and rubs damp spruce branches into his clothing it is raining. Having left the canoe overturned last evening the canoe is dry at least to start his trip.

While paddling, he closes in on every protruding stump that could be a moose. At the end of the lake, he follows the creek for two hundred metres before leaving the aluminium canoe's rain-driven drone and setting out on foot.

The newly tied plastic sheets, which serve as a roof over the hide, reverberate like a drum with the thumping of the rain. With his father's thoughts on controlling scent, he pulls out a plastic vinegar bottle from his pack and relieves his bladder. Then he goes back to listening and looking. Every black accumulation in the vast expanse has to be checked. His eyes scan slowly from left to right and then back again. When he thinks of how the moose so often creep up on the hunter's blind side, he slowly shifts to check behind. Every hour he climbs down, walks over marsh grass thirty metres, and makes a series of calls.

At eleven o'clock he munches peanuts and pulls out his copy of Hemingway's paperback *Farewell to Arms.* He scans the bush in between pages for three chapters; it's raining in that story too. Getting depressed, he tucks the book back in a plastic bag and returns it to his pack. At one o'clock he can no longer ignore the vibrating shiver up and down his back; he returns to camp.

After greeting Jacques and Bill, Gavin climbs out of his wet woollen clothes. He switches to a dry sweatsuit and pours himself a steaming coffee.

"Nothing at all," Jacques says, "S.T., they're not moving in this weather."

Gavin drinks three cups of coffee with his heaping plate of ragout. He finishes by layering strawberry jam over bread. Within an hour, he is dipping his paddle. At the hide, a series of crunches followed by hollow whacks has his heart jumping. He waits eagerly, until he must return due to the legal thirty-minute after sunset hunting limit. Gavin finds this time, basically, coincides with his inability to effectively use his rifle's sights.

On the water, Gavin keys his direction on the camp's faint illumination. The black water blurts and gurgles to his violent paddle thrusts. He knows Jacques will be worrying.

At camp, Jacques under the Coleman lantern's illumination flings three steaks into a giant sizzling pan. "*Sacrament*, where the 'ell's Gavin?" Jacques asks Bill in a harsh voice.

Bill, slicing onions, shrugs nonchalantly.

Jacques adjusts the pan so it is level, cuts the stove's draft and steps outside to check the lake. When he returns he says, "The lake is black with mist."

Five minutes later, toting a lantern, Jacques stabilizes the front of Gavin's canoe.

Gavin in response to Jacques' inquisitive look, says, "There was something ready to come out; I waited as long as I legally could."

They hunted through the rain on Sunday. No one saw game, but they all heard a wolf whining like a lonesome dog.

In the evening Jacques says, "S.T. I'm not going out tomorrow unless it stops raining. My clothes aren't dry from the previous day."

"Me neither," joins Bill.

Next morning it is cool, calm, and clear with a full moon when Gavin leaves the warm camp and walks into the semi-darkness. He carefully launches his canoe and paddles along the cap rock shore. Fifteen minutes later, he turns his head back when he hears a cow moose call. A flashlight beam back at camp puzzles him. Guess Jacques wants to bring the bull right to the camp, Gavin figures. Before Gavin reaches the end of the lake, he hears several exited yelps responding to Jacques' cow call back at camp. Soon whines and avaricious yelps echo across the mountains. Their primeval battle cries chill Gavin's bone marrow. Irrespective of expert claims, Gavin doesn't relish an encounter with an aroused wolf pack.

After landing, Gavin takes delicate steps, and many furtive glances in the dawn's breaking light, trudging his way to his hide and refuge from potential marauders.

Jacques and Bill are playing rummy when Gavin returns for lunch. Gavin shakes off his clothes and heats up a plate of wieners and beans. Sipping coffee, Gavin listens once more to the moans of a cow moose on his Walkman. He feels his call needs a more passionate terminal sigh. His dad always advised putting passion in a call and waiting for the bull to come out.

Back at his hide, he gives his call's revised version before climbing. In front, he scans the swollen creek that flows into the pond extending half the size of a football field. The easterly rain stops. There is an agitated silence for four minutes and then the north wind carries bursts of rain with machine gun rapidity. Spruce and cattails bend with each flurry of wind. Birch and aspen on the hillside sway in unison. The few remaining leaves vibrate free from their boughs and pirouette to their earthly rest.

At three o'clock Gavin gives another series of calls from the ground. In the hide, he stands and shifts behind the supporting spruce out of the wind's vengeance. At four o'clock, too stiff to climb down easily, he calls from the stand. He scans once more the open swamp at his left. Then as his gaze drifts straight ahead, he detects movement to his right. Turning slowly, his stare freezes on several spikes of reddish antlers. They project amongst alder branches thirty metres away.

The moose, with nose and rack tilted back, appears puzzled over the source of the call. Elevated ears start pivoting in all directions. Gavin eases off the safety, slowly rests the rifle on the restraining rail and waits. The moose steps out from the black spruce. Gavin aligns the sights of his 300 Savage slightly behind the front leg in the lower chest hoping to strike the heart. He tightens his trigger grip. The bull sprints twenty metres and drops.

Gavin studies the brush-obscured animal. After ten minutes, he clears the ammunition from his rifle and climbs down. He reloads his rifle and advances cautiously. The animal's eyes remain open and glazed which Gavin presumes means the animal is dead. He waits ten more minutes before approaching from behind its antlers. With no response after teasing the moose's ear with his rifle barrel, Gavin sighs in relief. After scrutinizing the animal for ten more minutes he touches it.

Now the moral responsibility for maximizing this mountain of meat confronts him. He knows it must be attended to immediately to preserve its quality, but he has been shivering for so long it is hard to concentrate. With his knife unsheathed and his folded saw-blade ready, he adjust the animals position as best he can. Gavin trims two y-shaped birch saplings and sharpens their bases. Next, he forces each limb away from the centre line with the forked strut anchored on the opposite side. He then ties cords to adjacent trees pulling the limbs even further apart and repositions his supports. With his knife, he frees the connective tissue from around the anus and ties it off. He cuts the skin from there through the pelvic and abdominal areas. Gavin carefully continues the slit through the abdomen and chest as far as possible. He guides the knife with blade facing up between his index and middle fingers. This procedure prevents the inadvertent puncture of the intestines with subsequent release of putrefying enzymes. He saws though the pelvic area and much of the sternum. He leaves one testicle to verify the sex, then ties off the entrances and exit from the bladder and removes it. Next, he ties off the digestive tract in the pelvic area and below the diaphragm, each in two places, and severs between the ties. This limits any contamination of meat from the intestines. With rubber gloves extending to his elbows, he drags out the abdominal intestinal tract slitting its connective tissue carefully where necessary. He severs attachments of the abdominal organs and regrets having to leave the cadmium concentrated liver, heart, and kidneys with the intestinal tract for local predators. He hauls these organs fifteen metres from the animal. Then he props open the emptied abdominal cavity with struts to hasten its cooling. This he learned years ago from his Mitchell-flying grandfather who claimed the quick drop of temperature reduces the chance of enzymes tainting the meat. When he pauses to assess what he has done, his shoulders convulse. He wipes his blade on the animal's fur, shoulders his pack and heads for camp.

Chapter 28

In their packs, they carry a block and tackle, extra rope, a small wood saw, axe, and a sharpening stone. Raindrops fry on the hot Coleman lantern as they paddle and hike to the moose. Jacques' first words on reaching the animal are, "Over this way Gavin." He guides Gavin's arm so the lantern shines on the animal's rack. Bill, intrigued with the animal, highlights the sheen of its fur by moving the beam of his flashlight back and forth.

Jacques says *"pardon"* and snatches the lantern from Gavin to be able to count the spines on the animal's rack. He then says, "That's a good one Gavin; it must be close to 900 pounds. Those tracks weren't that old after all, eh."

"Bill probes the animal's mouth and lower biting teeth. He reminds Gavin of his biology laboratory instructor who surveyed the dead white rat's features for what seemed like twenty minutes before wielding the dissecting scalpel.

"We better get moving Bill or we'll be 'ere all night," Jacques says. Bill reluctantly straightens but doesn't take his eyes or his flashlight off the sleek black fur that blends into white around the animal's legs.

They all pry on the moose's right front leg to shift it to a better working position but they can't budge it. Jacques secures the block and tackle to a tree, and they move the animal to a less obstructed area to clear the chest cavity. Bill, who has been shivering with each burst of wind, tears birch bark from a windfall, hacks at an old pine stump, and starts a fire.

Jacques finds the bending point of each lower leg and anchors it while Gavin cuts through its tendons. Then Gavin goes into a spruce copse and cuts three seven-metre long trees. He strips the branches, severs their tops, and then ties them in a tripod with a pulley lashed to the connection. They then slide the poles closer together above the moose's hind legs. With each person moving a pole, they edge the tripod to the desired height.

Jacques pauses again to hold a flaming twig over a freshly stocked pipe bowl while Gavin enlarges the gouge through the Achilles tendon of each hind limb. Bill, after tapering both ends of a sturdy freshly cut pole, threads the ends through each of the tendon notches and binds each leg to the strut. Bill calls this strut with the two hocks tied to it the gambrel stick and he and Gavin hoist the animal with the block and tackle.

Jacques knocks the half lit tobacco into the fire and says, "Let's wait until daylight to skin it, that fur will protect the meat until we can look after it properly."

"Good idea, it's near midnight," Bill says and adds, "The wolves won't touch it with all the human scent, besides they prefer guts."

Gavin looks at the suspended animal with some anxiety then dumps the contents of the plastic vinegar bottle in a circle around the animal and packs his equipment.

A howling wolf wakes Gavin in the night; he wonders if they are feasting on his moose.

A dusting of snow covers the brush when they walk to the canoe next morning. Gavin smashes the shore-ice with the handle of his paddle and they launch the canoe. Later each footfall on the trail causes the frozen earth to groan.

Behind the moose, on the southeast perimeter of the swamp, the sun sparkles through the spruce boughs. The black-brown moose hangs forlornly. Fresh snow powders the fur. Small animal tracks weave in and out of the discarded abdominal contents. Gavin sees no sign of wolves. They lower the moose to working height and Jacques starts skinning.

Gavin, by alternating between a knife and saw, separates the animal into eight manageable sections. Jacques wraps cheesecloth around the eight hunks of bush-beef.

"Now the fun starts, *n'est ce pas?*" Jacques says.

For the first trip, Jacques balances a hind ham on his shoulder. Bill straps a hunk to the horizontal projection of his aluminium-framed rucksack, while Gavin slings a slab of brisket on top of the padding of his personal flotation device.

At camp, they hang the meat on a beam between two trees using large *s*-shaped metal hooks. They spread a plastic sheet above it.

Next morning Jacques says, "I'll take the gear back to the truck and then come back for the moose and the canoe, if you two carry the meat to the main river. It's more complicated using boats than those guys who 'unt from their trucks. But they miss 'alf the fun."

"I'll be happy once we get the loaded boat and canoe above the rapids," Gavin chuckles.

In Sturgeon Falls, Jacques sprinkles the meat with black pepper to discourage flies and hangs it in his unheated shed. He has it butchered three days later.

Back in Sudbury, in returning Tanner's call to Ottawa, Gavin says, "Yes, 1985 was a good year in spite of its miserable beginning." After relating his hunting adventures, Gavin says, "I'll save you a roast."

Gavin now has his sights on the Commonwealth Games in Edinburgh, Scotland next summer.

With an attainable goal, financial support from the government, and an ample supply of lean protein, life for him should be straightforward. However, for the first time since getting the running bug, he loses his zest for training. Ten-kilometre runs each morning, twenty minutes on the swimming pool trampoline at lunch hour, and another fast paced workout in late afternoon leave him irritable and vowing to chuck it all.

He cuts his total running in half and goes back to bench stepping. He climbs, with an eight-pound sand bag draped around his neck, for eight consecutive minutes. It is an attempt to simulate the duration of his race.

Hearing details of Lisa's study on postmenopausal women's respiratory capacities does little to prompt Gavin's calls to London. Without further eligibility, he has no reason to train with the varsity athletes. He feels the varsity competitors, have lost their drive since Tanner's departure.

When he flubs his first accounting test, Gavin writes to the Ministry about trap line openings. They demand he take a trapping course, and he changes his mind.

In December, on completion of a trampoline workout, he sees Tanya taking measurements on swimmers. "What's up Tan?" he asks.

"I'm picking up data on stragglers who missed the main assessment in my study." When Tanya raises her left hand to measure a triceps skin fold, Gavin's heart loses its moorings, and his guts turn to water. He swallows hard and says, "I see you're wearing a sparkler. Do I know the guy?"

"Langdon, Frederic Langdon from Toronto, remember?"

Hell no, he thinks to himself, but to her he says, "Oh! Congratulations. Have you set a date?"

"A year next Christmas when I finish my program."

"Where you going to live?"

"Toronto, Frederic's with his dad in the insurance business."

"He's all set then isn't he?"

"He seems to be."

Gavin's solar plexus replays the same sensation he had when his car spun out of control in a snowstorm and tumbled into a ditch.

Although many evenings he debates the sanity of his desire to be a runner, the demands of the day crowd out negative thoughts. From the first step out of bed until he kicks off his shoes at night, every minute is accounted for. A professor who arrives late or talks off topic rattles him. He has little patience with advising varsity runners who constantly seek the easy way to the top. He retreats into a world of schoolwork, training, and the occasional flying lesson.

By June of '86 he has kept the blues at bay enough to pass his accounting exams, average 120 kilometres of snappy running a week, and claim a berth on the Canadian Team for the Commonwealth Games in Edinburgh, Scotland.

Chapter 29

The 1986 Commonwealth Games Team assembles at the Cambridge Hotel close to the Lester B. Pearson International Airport. Team dress for travel is the same as for the marching in ceremonies: ties and jackets. Minutes before the last airport shuttle is scheduled to leave, Gavin can't remember how to knot a tie. Several other athletes scramble in the hallways searching for anyone who can. Canadians attending American universities, where ties on athletic trips are mandatory, become instantly popular.

After a turbulent night over the Atlantic, the team arrives at five in the morning Glasgow time. The athletes, when seeking Edinburgh buses, are intercepted by television crews. One interviewer asks, "What do you think of the African countries pulling out of the Games?"

The moment Gavin turns to trace the voice's source, a microphone appears in his face. "Look, I came to run as fast as I can for the 3,000-metre steeplechase. I race whoever shows up; simple as that." Gavin keeps walking but notices the reporter frowns and repeats his same statement to the next group.

It is rainy, cold, and dark, when Gavin and Jake board the third of five chartered buses for Edinburgh. Along the sombre countryside, Gavin expects to see Macbeth's witches.

Approaching Edinburgh, the driver points to a castle growing out of a cliff. "Edinburgh Castle," he slurs, as though everyone knows its total significance. Winding into the downtown area, the operator relates how an early king's promenade became known as the Royal Mile. Minutes later the man at the wheel remarks, "The Palace of Holyrood, which we are now passing, will serve as the Queen's residence during these Games."

"It's a bit like stepping back into history," Jake says to Gavin.

"Yes, a history choked with intrigue I understand."

Before unpacking, Gavin peers out the rear window of the room he shares with Jake in the Pollock Halls of Residence. He sees a steep, scrub grass mountain, topped with an odd rock formation resembling a saddle. He remembers someone saying, this is where the legendary King Arthur did his thinking. Gavin makes a mental note to run up the trail the day after his race.

Closer, perhaps thirty metres away, an old rock wall with a strand of barbed wire serves as the rear barrier of the village. Two cats, disdainful of the barbs, frolic about. At street level, a service road leads to the adjacent cafeteria.

In the room, the duvet on Gavin's upper bunk looks cozy. He debates a moment whether to stay up and stretch the day even longer or nap. Gavin climbs the ladder.

Jake bursts back into the room, scans his short pants, and says, "If it takes foreign bagpipes two weeks to acclimatize in Edinburgh weather before a piping competition, how long will it take two track and field athletes to reverse their seasons?"

Gavin rolls over to see Jake changing back to his full-length pants.

When not training, Gavin plays hearts, reads Scottish newspapers or takes advantage of the next room's video shows. An enterprising swimmer has rented a VCR. Except for a team reception with the Queen, Gavin stays put. He finds the advantage of not having to walk far for meals offset by the growling trucks delivering at all hours. The pervasive odour of vegetable soup kills his interest in anything resembling broth.

A week of only moderate training and no other stresses makes Gavin restless and ready. On race day, he arrives at Meadowbank Stadium warmup track early. Slowly he increases his activity. Forty minutes later an official with a sergeant-major voice summons the athletes into the stadium.

Gavin's slow and deliberate breathing would rank him a model of composure, but his mind is a jumble—okay, I'm coming! You don't have to shout, he says to himself as he joins the sergeant-major's line. When he enters Meadowbank Stadium, he dubs it patchwork palace. The stadium seating additions seemed to reflect the fluctuating prices of concrete, steel, and wood rather than an overall design. Thoughts reverberate in Gavin's mind: Geez it's packed! My God, the fans have the wave going; those wooden bleachers won't take it. There's Hackney, ah, he never has two good races back to back, I can forget about him; Nelson—he's tough but listen to that gravelly cough. He can't stop barking long enough to tie his shoes. Wonder if this misty rain will turn to snow before the starter learns to reload his pistol. Is it the Queen or Thatcher in the Royal Box today? My laces—I didn't tighten them enough after my warmup—no, no, they're okay. Do I have time for a leak? I wish I did more speed work this year. The last lap will be a blitz—Nah. Nah. I'm ready. God it's cold! No wonder so many Scotsman end up in Canada; the middle of summer and you need a snowmobile suit to keep warm. Where is that stadium clock? It must be after three o'clock by now. I'm going to join those Aussies tonight; they never stop partying. That man, talking to the starter, has a woollen scarf around his neck in the middle of summer. Could you imagine going down Elm Street in Sudbury looking like that this time of year? Keep control—be a vicious animal on the last lap. Finally, the starter has figured out how to load the gun! How do they appoint their officials? Hope my ankle's okay!

Gavin has a clean start and relaxes for 400 metres. When athletes have to deliberately cut their stride to avoid stepping on those in front, Gavin senses he has to go, or risk everything on his weak sprint finish. Besides, he is anxious to show the world the fitness he has sacrificed so much to achieve. He bounds into the headwind and leads the pack.

At the end of five laps, he is five meters clear of the field and the lap clock indicates fast intermediate times. Where are they? He asks himself with proud wonder. Could he actually steal the Commonwealth Gold this easily? The crowd, however, unleashes a scream as he bolts into the last lap. Nelson's throaty breathing reaches his ears. Like a cornered animal, Gavin summons his last charge of epinephrine. A barrage of unrefined movements spring forth. He holds his pursuers off during the wind-aided backstretch and over the final water jump. The crowd's howl, however, warns him the wolves are posturing for the kill. A gust assails his leap over the last barrier 60 metres from the finish. His lead leg clears, but the trail leg touches. Gavin's two-stride stumble allows one athlete to his left and two on his right to pass. Goose pimpled, he musters a counter attack. Like an animal after a mortal wound, he flounders to the finish. Gavin drops to his hands and knees on the infield's wet grass until his vision clears.

With a glance at the electronic results, he says, "Wow, fourth in 8:27.12." A smile invades his face and his brain's motor area gains control of his limbs. With his attendant rushing to keep up, he skips across to the protected lower level of the stadium. Gavin squats, takes off his spiked shoes and climbs into his sweat bottoms. Then, with a sprightly gait, he heads toward the throng of coaches, athletes, and officials in the warmup area.

Ahead of him he notices Nelson, the winner, talking with a grey haired gentleman dressed in navy blue jacket and grey flannels. He overhears the older man say, "Jolly good show! That impetuous Canadian set you up to unleash your kick."

"He sure did, thanks Mr. Gladbourough," Nelson says, his eyes sparkling until his face again contorts into another cough.

"You'll be in the money in Seoul if you mind that respiratory problem."

"Right," Nelson responds flashing his white teeth.

"So, I'm an impetuous Canadian," Gavin repeats and bites his lower lip— "Could Tanner's advice have helped, did I tip my hand too soon?"

A hand touches Gavin's shoulder. The Canadian distance coach hands him a printout of his running times. Gavin ponders why he took the bait so early. A more even pace would have left him more for the finish. Still, it is a personal best under blustery conditions.

That evening, Gavin joins the Aussies taking advantage of the sponsors' brown cream ale. When Gavin explains that he lives northwest of Toronto, he has trouble convincing the Australians that the snow leaves the ground for more than two months a year. Gavin exchanges his rain suit and two Canadian golf shirts for an Australian steeplechaser's sweat-suit. When a couple of Canadians leave early, Gavin joins them. During the ride, the comments by the Englishman he overheard after the race irk him again. Could it be true, he ponders? Does he have to hear it from someone else before he believes his own coach?

The next day, with both finished their events Jake and Gavin visit *The Scotsman* newspaper. Gavin contemplates why a daily owned for so long by a Canadian Lord Beaverbrook would buy newsprint from Norway instead of Canada. In the layout area, several people work elbow to elbow. Gavin considers how miserable it would be for him to toil in such proximity with people holding forth different perspectives.

In the sports department, Gavin scans a photograph of the men's 100-metre start from the afternoon's competition. "Look at that," Gavin says to Jake, "the Scottish athlete made a false start and no one recalled him."

"Yes," Jake replies chuckling, "it's easier to recognize it in a photograph than it is to call it on the spot."

Gavin looks at the name Gosford on a door as they leave *The Scotsman*, and wonders if he has any relations here. His father mentioned Goslings had ancestors from Berwick, a small town on the border of England and Scotland. Berwick, his dad related, was still at war with Napoleon; for having declared war as an independent entity, Berwick had never resolved peace with France after being amalgamated with Scotland.

Retracing steps through stone passageways in Edinburgh Castle conjures up terror. Later in the city, a guide points to a mark on the pavement where workers built the last execution gallows. It being the practice to do the hanging at the scene of the crime, the scaffold was built here. The window overlooking a pond used by the sickly Robert Louis Stevenson brings back images of *grand'mère* reading *Treasure Island* to him on special weekends. Stevenson, Gavin muses, concocted his adventures; he is living his.

A special boat tour to the Bonnie Banks of Clyde didn't uncover the Lochness Monster, but it did reveal water-skiers in July in wet suits. Oh to be in Canada now that summer's here, tingles in his mind.

After the Closing Ceremonies, nonresidents began closing zippers on over-stuffed travel bags. With the visitors' departure, the omnipresent roses lost many an envious stare.

Chapter 30

"Gavin, your preparation was right, but when it's windy you'll have to hold back," Tanner says over the telephone. "Jump them when you feel you can carry it to the end. I could tell, on the TV flash, your uncoordinated movements courted trouble before you nicked the barrier."

"It's possible; who knows?" Gavin replies, and stretches his arm for a moment.

Tanner continues, "For the time being, do the flat races in the meets we planned and the steeplechase at the Ontario Championships. After that pick up any road races that interest you. In November, our goal will be next July's World University Games in Zagreb.

"Sounds fine," Gavin replies.

"Your time in the steeplechase, incidentally, renews Sports Canada funding for another year. See you."

After the call Gavin figures with the prize money now offered in road races, he will be able to add to his fourteen hours with the Cessna. At eighty bucks a spin it isn't cheap. Eventually he is pointing for a commercial license since fly-in services are in demand.

Cutting brush on the cross-country ski trails at minimum wage gives Gavin out-of-doors work and flexible hours. Evenings he stretches back in the residence common room with the first newspaper or magazine in sight. At ten o'clock, the three evenings a week the university pub is open, he shoots pool.

In the third successive day of a heat wave, Gavin goes to the pub early. He notices a couple exuberantly sharing their day's activities. At that moment, he feels nostalgic for the carefree life he had before being galvanized by running. Being a high-powered athlete pleases him; he doesn't begrudge its physical cost. Nevertheless, when the intoxication of racing is far off, he feels ensnarled in a bleak existence. Periodic accusations by friends that he leads a dull life provoke an indulgent smile; such people, he figures, never filled Visa forms at a gas bar for a living.

As he reflected his way to the bottom of his first draft, the giggles from the lovers at the next table force a reconsideration of his decision. Has he denied himself too much? What has all his running achieved? Sure, in his event, he is amongst the top thirty in the world, but who cares? Yet, he knows the glow he harbours of ranking with the best steeplechasers in the Commonwealth, charms his every hour. While savouring a fresh draft, he frowns on noticing the same couple leaving the pub arms entwined.

An hour later, Gavin overhears Ted the pub security guard ask his supervisor, "May I knock off early, I'd like to check the action at the Coulson? Things are quiet here."

"Go ahead, I'll close up," the burly manager replies.

"Could I get a lift down town with you Ted?" Gavin asks.

At the Coulson Hotel Lounge, Ted greets his chum who is a bouncer. Ted and Gavin are ushered to seats close to the entertainment stage.

Within seconds, a well-endowed, mini-skirted brunet is at Ted's elbow; she teases him while she takes his order.

"Gina, this is Gavin; he's a runner," Ted says.

Gavin and Gina exchange nods.

Gavin's attention returns to the stage where Mona, a frizzy-haired, acrobatic dancer, is doing back handsprings. Gavin is on the edge of his seat; he murmurs, "She must have been quite a gymnast in high school." When Ted doesn't respond, Gavin realizes Ted has more than passing interest in the sparsely clad Gina. After the next peeler's series of back-bend overs exhibit a tantalizing twist of her scant pubic hair, the main lights reappear.

Gavin straightens his chair and clears his throat. Ted, like a private detective, never loses sight of his prey. Gavin eventually turns to investigate Ted's attraction. He sees Gina accompanied by the frizzy-haired gymnast, Mona, approaching their table. Gavin smiles, noticing Mona has changed into white jean shorts and a blue denim sleeveless top. Both girls respond to the boys' attention. Cutting through clouds of cigarette smoke, and ignoring whistles and rowdy chatter, the girls arrive at the boys' table.

"Y'all havin' a good time?" Mona asks, and stands beside Gavin's chair.

"Quite a show, where'd you learn your gymnastics?" Gavin asks.

"Belonged to a club in Toronto while my dad was back-up quarterback for the Argos." She then bends down and whispers to Gavin, "Stay with Ted after ma last show and I'll tail ya mor', much mor'."

Gavin smiles and doesn't answer. Ted gives Gavin a slight nod. Gavin says to himself, why not.

After closing, Gavin waits on the street with the two girls while Ted gets his Camaro. When everyone gets in Ted says, "How about having a bonfire at our cottage on Long Lake, no one's around and the fridge is full."

"Sounds fine, but y'all decide," The gymnast replies with a hint of adventurousness in her voice. She then shifts her position so she is almost entirely on Gavin's lap.

Ted drives west of the city, turns onto a secondary road and then over gravel. When they make a right turn onto a grass-centred road Gavin notices a car at a distance behind. His thoughts stray from the lubricity of the female in his arms, to the wonder that anyone else would concoct a private party at this hour.

After parking, Ted leads Gina, Mona, and Gavin down three flights of moonlit, wooden steps to the camp's entrance. Considerable bush separates the neighbouring cottages on both sides.

When Ted pauses to open the door with his key, Mona says, "I'd just love a swim raight now, it's been so sweltering."

"Go ahead, I'll bring some wood down for a fire by the shore," Ted says.

"Yawl goin' a join me," Mona asks.

"Sure," Gavin responds.

They both strip on the dock beside an old Jacuzzi. Mona stacks her attire neatly on the corner of the dock then climbs down the ladder and swims around under the diving board. She does a slick surface dive under the board and then climbs back on the dock.

"Seems safe," Mona says. The moon shimmers from her wet body as she does a front one-and-a-half, and a semi-wide-open back.

"Hey, not bad." Gavin shouts.

After Mona does three more dives, Gavin joins her in a swim further from shore. Mona slips along like a beaver making barely a ripple. They are forty metres from shore when they hear a crashing of metal, five thuds and much tinkling of glass from high up on Ted's laneway. They hear wheels spinning over gravel and see light beams streak through the trees. They stroke back to shore, dress scantily, climb steps, and see Ted picking bits of broken glass from below a dented hood and crashed-in, front headlight.

Mona groans, "Those punks just caint leave me alone kin they?"

Ted glares at Mona's almost flat hair for five seconds and slowly returns to gathering the remaining loose objects from the ground.

Gina says, "Kin you git us back Ted, before we have any more trouble?"

With one headlight functioning, Ted returns Mona to Larch Street, drops Gavin on Notre Dame and drives Gina to Coniston. In Gavin's walk to residence, he ponders his break-up with Tanya. Although it is devastating, he realizes he has had to give running his all or he would never have forgiven himself.

August passes with two track meets, two lucrative road races, three flying lessons, and a stagnant social life.

On Labour Day, Gavin picks up a ringing telephone.

"Hi, it's Tanya," Gavin swallows hard. "Look," she says, "I can't get through on Janet's line to tell her I want to share an apartment with her. I must contact her immediately before she gets someone else. Would you mind talking to her for me?"

"You returning to Laurentian, Tanya?"

"Yes, my new advisor insists my thesis needs refining. I didn't control heart rates as a motivating factor with grip strength measures. Probably take another year."

"How's Frederic?"

"He wants me to drop it. Says I won't need my degree when we're married."

"Oh," Gavin replies.

"See Janet soon as you can, would you?

"I'll do that. Where can you be reached?"

"I've been living at Frederic's since finishing work on Manitoulin Island."

Gavin sighs to himself and dutifully copies the number.

A week later, it's a sweltering day when Tanya arrives with her father. Besides a totally loaded Audi there is a bicycle attached to the roof rack. On Tanya's first trip, she eases down two suitcases at Gavin's door and knocks. While waiting, she tucks in a lock and glances at her legs glistening from the effort.

"Thanks for talking with Janet," she says.

"No problem," Gavin says and gives her a brotherly hug. When a ringless finger catches his eye, his heart triples its rhythm. "Where's your sparkler? Have you—"

"No, we're still engaged. It's just—I don't know what to say."

Noticing her luggage and flushed face, Gavin asks, "Could I help?"

"That would be great. Dad drove; I sold my car. We're at the back of the building."

"I'll grab a shirt," Gavin says.

When they arrive, Thoburn extends a well-tanned hand, "It's been a long time—you had an excellent race at the Commonwealth."

"I was happy with it," Gavin replies, grinning.

"Speaking about Games, I'm doing some video work for Toronto's bid on the '96 Olympics. I'll be catching international soccer shots this September with the Canadian Team in Mexico."

"Good for you! Too bad Toronto is against a city like Athens. The celebration of the 100th anniversary of the Modern Olympics in Greece is bound to carry a lot of weight."

"Perhaps, but with the political turmoil there you never know; Toronto could luck out."

"By the way, how's your health?"

"Just great! I'm up to an hour of walking-jogging five days a week."

"Wonderful!" Gavin replies and he bends over to tug out Tanya's '82 blue Commonwealth team duffle bag from the Audi trunk. It conjures up the evening they shared when she returned from Australia.

An hour later when Tanya guides her mountain bike up in the elevator with him and gets off at her floor she nudges him saying, "Thanks Gavin," with a twinkle he hasn't seen for some time.

"See you," Gavin responds with a forced air of flippancy.

Gavin's placing in the Commonwealth Games gives him a temporary status at Christmas and a confirmed spot in May for the '87 World University Team for Zagreb.

On the sixth of July, the Canadian Team rendezvous in Toronto and flies overnight to Zurich. They then continue on to sticky Zagreb. Tired athletes stand for hours getting temporary accreditation; those who submitted incomplete data on forms confront serious processing delays. When Gavin notices a shorter queue in an unusual line, he plays dumb and gets a speedier accreditation; other team members follow him.

Canadian Track Team quarters are on the third floor of "C" residence in the Sava Athletes' Village. Limp tree leaves border the building. Gavin's window faces the main street; a musical combo plays United States tunes from the fifties. A team dressed in yellow shorts and blue tops shuffles by in sandals. Up the street, by a willow grove, a delegation of tie and jacket-clad athletes hoists the Rising Sun amongst the other drooping flags in the three o'clock heat. Gavin clamps his window open, pulls the curtain across and crawls into bed.

Jake wakes Gavin three hours later when he stumbles in with his bags. Jake, after trying in vain to trace his poles, leaves the airport with assurances his missing equipment will be delivered in the morning.

Gavin, now refreshed, decides to run before it gets dark. He interrupts the flirting of a couple of translators at the main desk to ask, "Where might someone run that is free from traffic and people?"

"For running," the daintily-featured translator purses her lips and says, "The banks of the Sava River. It is close; I will show you."

From the front of the building, she points at the gate to go through, the street to cross, and the bridge to go under.

Gavin starts at a moderate pace. The strange sounds of a language he doesn't understand mystify him. He meets hundreds running who were, no doubt, given the same advice on a private place to exercise.

He strides under one busy bridge, up and over another, and then into a park. It differs from a Canadian city park for no grass is cut here, but there are benches and fountains. The pond in the centre is two meters lower than usual judging from the striations on its sand banks. A withered faced man stares at a red bobber floating in brown water.

Grief! Imagine fishing in mud. That man would go crazy in clear Canadian lakes. The fisherman's blue tent is on the other side of the pond. Thirty minutes later Gavin retraces his steps.

After showering, Gavin scans the Village. It's noisier than Edinburgh. Disco music drowns the usual hustle of excited young people. The U.S.S.R. athletes are next to the outdoor disco centre; Gavin doesn't envy them.

Gavin joins Jake for dinner. They choose an elevated semi-open cafeteria where the breeze carries the heat away from the steam table. Small pictures of a pig, a cow, and a fish present the main evening choices.

After practice next day, Gavin joins the interpreter's tour of the downtown area. He visits a Gothic 13th-14th century sandstone cathedral. Its external statues look to be crying sand tears as they fight a losing battle to the pollutants.

He learns of the struggles the early ecclesiastics on one side of a creek had with the artisans on the other. A bronze sculpture in the marketplace depicts the circle of life. He admires the fit-looking bodies in all the represented ages. The slouch of an older sculpted man reminds him of his grandfather. Behind the bronze work, a wrinkled lady wearing a red, checked kerchief uses a broom made of tied branches.

Returning, Gavin picks up the *Universiade News* at the security gate. It is written in Yugoslavian, French, and English. The Games' slogan, "The Youth of the World for a World of Peace" headlines the front page. Other articles note the Secretary General of the United Nations, Mr. Perez de Cuellar, will welcome the 5-billionth inhabitant of the earth in a Zagreb hospital; a rock group called the Elektricni Orgazam will entertain the athletes tonight; there are 7,000 athletes from 128 countries. On the back page Gavin reads, the Village authorities have issued condoms to all athletes in an attempt to control the foreign invasion of the Aids virus. A mistake has occurred, however, with the allotment for the 500 U.S.S.R athletes. Their shipment was inadvertently sent to the 12-member New Zealand team. Three days later, the Soviet manager informs the New Zealand delegation of the mistake. The New Zealand Chef-de-Mission's response is, "Regrettably the lads have used them all."

Gavin falls asleep at ten with the newspaper across his chest. He wakes at midnight and tosses the newspaper to the floor.

Before coming to Zagreb, Gavin worked with Tanner on an intensive heat adaptation program. Since arriving, he has adopted the routine of sharp, short, quality running in the early mornings. Having gained heat acclimatization before coming, Gavin now gives his body a chance to adapt to other changes. He does familiarize himself with the water jump approach in the stadium. Twice he trains at the same time of day as his race will be held. This action is to get accustomed to any glare he might get from the sun reflecting from steeplechase trough water. Gavin notices his rivals working exceptionally hard. Gavin smiles remembering Tanner saying, "It's too late to do much once you get to Zagreb." One thing Gavin didn't take into account was his difficulty in communicating with the officials.

Escorted to the assembly area on the day of the final, Gavin needs to go to the toilet. He almost breaks into a tantrum when a policeman insists he doesn't need to go. Gavin ignores abusive language and uses the adjacent facilities.

He remembers Tanner saying, "Don't let anything interfere with your concentration before the race." Gavin regains his composure and thanks the stone-faced policeman on returning.

When he lines up with the thirteen other qualifiers on this muggy afternoon, he knows the oppressive heat will prevent a fast time. Gavin plans to use Tanner's tactics of waiting. No one wants to set pace. Gavin stays on the inside, a box forms around him. He doesn't mind on the second and third laps but on the fourth he signals that he wants out by pointing. The Cuban athlete beside him doesn't move. Gavin eases out imperceptibly; he takes 100 metres to be clear of Juan Bautista. Then like a human catapult, he breaks free from the pack; vexed from the confinement, he gallops over barriers and water jumps saying to himself catch me if you can. The crowd roar approval; action delights them this sultry day. A minute later, the clamour turns to a hush and then a building roar. Gavin knows something serious is happening. He decides to squelch his pursuer immediately with his own acceleration. Attacking footsteps fade; the bluff works! Thank God! Gavin says to himself, for he has nothing in him with fifty metres to go. Five seconds later a crescendo of voices returns. Gavin appreciates this can mean only one thing—someone is still there. Like a boxer trying for a last second knock out, Gavin punches his arms hoping to ignite his weary legs, but Alexei Vasilov of the U.S.S.R. lunges over the finish line three centimetres ahead of him.

Chapter 31

The hymn of the World University Games floats through Dinamo Stadium for the 3,000-metre steeplechase victors. Gavin beams thinking he and his coach have finally worked it out. He regrets another crisis at the Canadian Track and Field Association office has kept Tanner from making the trip. Gavin wonders if Tanya is watching and whether she has made up her mind about Frederic.

On the athletes' bus to residence a Yugoslavian bursts into song. Gavin grins, his heart sings along but his lips know not the words. His spirit is still cavorting with the Greek Gods he met two years ago in Athens.

Team manager Sandstrom asks the driver to stop at a pub on Avenija VIII outside the Village. He then clutches Gavin's arm and leads him off the bus with seven other members of the Canadian team.

With his stein filled, Sandstrom stands, wipes potato chip remnants from his mustache, and says, "Gosling you knocked their jocks off with that burst, here's to ya." During the evening, the Canadian group stand with a boisterous toast every time the TV replays the 3,000-metre steeplechase final.

After the third Canadian ruckus, a gentleman under a Crocodile Dundee hat, celebrating the 4th place Australian finish in the walk, yells, "Hey, Gosling! What's a Canada goose sound like?"

Heads lift from the Canadian table and eyes drift to the Dundee hat. The Aussie, after an appropriate pause, tilts his head, flaps his bent arms, and utters, "Honk, honk, eh!"

"Not bad for a wallaby, eh!" Sandstrom replies.

Next day with his eyes still sparkling, Gavin watches his teammates compete. The only shade in the athletes' area is at the top of the stadium. If he sits there, the result's board is out of view. The Games' flame at the section's lowest seats can be felt thirty metres from its base. Gavin chooses a spot in between. For the first time in months he can lean back and eat his fill of ice-cream bars while his memory—between events on the track—replays each stage of yesterday's race.

Back at Sava Village, Gavin has a note attached to his door, "Check with Sandstrom." It is a telex inviting him to compete in Zurich the following weekend.

"They evidently want a rematch between you and Alexei Vasilov," Sandstrom says with a smirk.

"What about it?" Gavin asks Tanner in a call back to Ottawa.

"By all means, Zurich is noted for being cool and calm. If conditions are right, blast it from the gun."

Gavin joins other elite athletes from many nationalities on the air trek to Zurich. The sight of the Alps and the view of a large lake from his hotel window give him a sense of tranquility. He spoils himself for three days on a menu normally reserved for heads of state. Grinding the soles off four pairs of training shoes this year has been well worth it, he chuckles.

Buoyant from success and proud of his ascendancy to the world elite, Gavin takes full advantage of the cool Zurich evening. He leads from the gun and hacks eleven seconds from his best time in winning. Vasilov finishes third.

Life back home immediately becomes confusing. Promoters, who have ignored him, suddenly become his supposed best friends. Gavin, in desperation, refers his new pursuers to Tanner. Following three outstanding performances in non-steeplechase Canadian races and one steeplechase in London, England on a weekend, Tanner closes the book on Gavin's 1987 season. Training strategy for next year's Seoul Olympics takes priority.

The lustre of Gavin's accomplishments, like the summer sun, fades with the approach of autumn. Gavin is once more forced to reflect on where he is going in life. Although he has climbed that magic podium of international success, he has done nothing to balance his life outside of track. He loses himself in an aviation manual one day and then tries reading all the supplementary materials for a course on the next. He debates telephoning Jacques about going for another moose hunt. Eventually, fear of twisting an ankle prevents him. He does, however, write to his mother apologizing for his rude comments the day she left him in North Bay to pursue a new life in the Yukon.

In the Muskokas at Reginald Thoburn's winterized home, Tanya and Carolyn join their father on the Labour Day weekend.

"God, how refreshing to put your feet up," Tanya says to her dad after he hands her a cup of coffee on the porch. She continues, "Feel that crispness in the air; look how the sun brings out the red and yellow colours in those hardwoods. I've never appreciated this view so much. You know, in spite of living in a gorgeous home in Toronto, I anticipate that subway shake every ten minutes. Frederic insists, considering the price of accomodation, that we stay in his parents'guest apartment for the time being. But I can't stand Mrs. Langdon; she, she—oh I detest her company." Tanya thrusts her palms up and then drops her arms to the sides of her chair, raises, crosses, and supports her legs on the stool in front of her and lets her chin sag.

Carolyn, who has cleared the breakfast dishes, comes out and joins them with a fresh Silex of coffee, "Another, Tan?"

"Half' will do thanks."

"How are things with you and Frederic?" Mr. Thoburn asks softly.

"I'm not sure. When he comes back from work he's tired; he doesn't even want to go sailing. At parties he's exciting to be with; he remembers names, cracks jokes and knows what's exciting in every city in North America. Frederic has a way with everyone he meets of prompting conversation. But when the rum hits him, I have to guide him to the car." Tanya stares blankly into her coffee cup.

"Well, well, is this a stage he's going through in coping with the business world?" Mr. Thoburn asks.

"I would like to think so, but I don't. There's something driving him that he can't control. Frederic is similar to

Gavin in many ways, but Gavin attacks his restlessness directly: he increases training, takes an additional course, or more flying lessons. Frederic, on the other hand, doesn't know where to begin."

"Speaking about Gavin, he had quite a run in Zagreb—almost stole the show, "Mr. Thoburn says. He lifts his head and grins the way he did when he watched the race on television.

"Yes, I sent him a note. He looked so natural during his interview."

"So Tanya, you working now?" Carolyn asks.

"No looking."

"You've been at school this long and all you're doing is looking? God! I guess I didn't make a mistake not continuing."

"Unexpectedly, my advisor offered me a job as research assistant this year but I couldn't accept with marriage at Christmas."

"What the hell difference does that make on your plans? Don't you intend to do something?" Carolyn asks, squinting. After a minute's silence Carolyn continues, "Why don't you drop that jerk and corral that mad trapper?"

Tanya swallows hard and her cheeks flush. She lowers her legs and eases her weight to the front of her chair; she sucks in her upper lip. When her coffee cup jiggles, she places it back on the table. Tanya sits back in her seat, expires slowly, and when her hand becomes steady, she grips her mug again. Following two prolonged sips, she glances at her father who is still smothering a grin from Carolyn's comment. After sixty seconds of silence Tanya says, "That's it! You're right! I'm going to accept that job at Laurentian."

On the Tuesday after Labour Day, Tanya accepts her advisor's offer over the phone. She drives to Sudbury with her dad, and signs the two-year contract to measure the physical fitness of seniors in the Sudbury basin.

Mr. Thoburn in Sudbury uses his Betacam video camera to tape Gavin's training over the water jump and through the Simic trails. He is completing his feature on the preparation of ten Canadian Olympians. Thoburn also intends to use scenes of an eight-lane polyurethane track surrounded by birch and pine to portray Canada's natural settings for athletics in Canada to support the Olympic bid.

Gavin offers Tanya a place to stay until she finds an apartment. Tanya is still sharing Gavin's apartment when Gavin leaves for the Olympic Games in Seoul in September of 1988.

Chapter 32

It is 3:13 p.m., 30 September 1988 in Seoul, South Korea, and the Olympic 3,000-metre steeplechase will start in two minutes. Millions share this happening. In Los Angeles it is 11:13 p.m. the previous day; a University of California athlete adjusts his set searching for Matt Kelly the athlete who edged him out of a spot on the United States' team. At 1:13 a.m., Tanya, in a common room of the university residence in Sudbury, insists on holding the remote control even though she has inadvertently changed channels twice in the last five minutes. A nurse in Surrey, England wipes the sleep from her eyes, clears her throat, and gazes at the television screen. It is 6:13 a.m. and she is waiting for her cousin, Michael Nelson, to compete for Great Britain. At 9:13 a.m. in Kenya, the children in the school from which Julius Korir, the defending Olympic Champion has graduated, have two television sets in the hallways. In downtown Seoul, a ten-year-old, without home access to television, joins three older men in an electronics store on Chungmu-Ro watching this multifaceted event.

In the Olympic Stadium Andy Tanner examines his Seiko stopwatch, places it on his lap, and fumbles for a ballpoint pen. He settles for a pencil. When he starts writing, the abandoned stopwatch crashes to the concrete. In retrieving it, he jostles the lady in front, apologizes, and swears under his breath. Next, he breaks the pencil lead framing lap time columns.

Reginald Thoburn, in Seoul preparing video materials for Toronto's Olympic bid, takes shots of the crowd and threads his way to the photographers' dugout. Here his Beta cam video is poised five meters from the water jump, free from the sun's glare. Other photographers have also claimed prime vantage viewing and guard with extended elbows their cherished places.

At the Stadium top, seven members of the Jury of Appeal, dressed in traditional crimson jackets, check the competitors' list. Amongst those sequestered is the Canadian, Richard Pearce, an executive with the Royal Bank of Canada. Pearce, a former international decathlete, coordinated the '76 Olympic decathlon officials. His expeditious handling of seeding in this complicated multi-event led the International Amateur Athletic Federation to sponsor his visit to Seoul, some months earlier.

The Korean hostess, while carrying a tray of coffee and sweets, recognizes Richard and sets her tray on a fold-down table beside him. Mr. Gladbourough, from Great Britain, chairman of the Jury, frowns and grumbles while he checks the start list. He leans forward, touches Pearce's shoulder and says, "Isn't that a Canadian in the final? Must've drawn easy heats to make it this far—mind, standards have slipped."

Pearce lowers his binoculars, rubs the back of his hand on each eyebrow, and says, "Sinking standards for sure when a lame limy like Nelson qualifies, eh." Pearce then glares through the binoculars and teases the fine adjustment back and forth, back and forth in viewing the starter's raised pistol.

On the track, Gavin keeps a constant chatter with himself—great I made it to the final without having to go flat out. I'll show those peering eyes what a Canadian bushwhacker can do. With the starter's final command, Gavin leans over the start line and remains motionless. He is one of fourteen poised to pounce.

Oblivious to the clamour of 100,000 spectators, Gavin bolts with the gun. A shoulder collides with his right arm and he tilts to avoid an obstructing hip. The crush eases when they hit the backstretch. Alexei Vasilov is in the lead.

Gavin remembers reading about this U.S.S.R. athlete, whose father became a master of sport through his 800-metre running and his mother achieved bronze medallist status in floor exercises. A Swedish journalist claimed Vasilov to be a child of the Olympics for he was born nine months after the '64 Games. Gymnastics and hill running dominated his early years. He reached national success as a youth in the 1,500-metre event. Switching to the steeplechase, he flourished as the European and World University Games' Champion. Powerful and lithe, he has his father's speed and his mother's dexterity. Gavin peers at the Soviet's supple body rhythmically loping over the barriers and indulges in a mental taunt: You may look good but Canadian Bill Crothers knocked your old man for a loop in '64 and I'm planning the same for you.

Gavin is in last place as they shift into the shade of the cavernous roof at the first water jump. A galaxy of flashes forces Gavin into taking stutter steps on approaching the barrier. Back in the sun he blinks three times with his eyes fixed on Vasilov. On the second lap Julius Korir from Kenya takes the lead. Korir changes his mind and the American, Kelly, moves up. The others hang together like a swarm of angry bees with Gavin a stride behind. He knows the world record will go if they maintain this pace and he senses they aren't ready to better eight minutes and six seconds. He remembers his dad's advice when calling moose—be patient until the animal presents itself. On successive laps Gavin checks the digital time display; the 3rd, 4th, and 5th laps are a trifle slower than the first two. Shifting wide of struggling athletes, Gavin moves into the pack and scans for more faltering runners. He is fifth with one lap to go and sees Vasilov's trail leg dragging over the obstacles. Kelly wobbles on each landing. Nelson, who told the press he twisted an ankle in the preliminary heats, shows no trace of limping, but his rib cage quivers haphazardly. It is only Korir who has the same poker face he had the first lap and scurries with reckless abandon.

"NOW!" Gavin screams at himself and releases a barrage of nerve impulses: knees punch higher, strides stretch longer, and arms whip savagely. Not without cost—within 200 metres of the finish, muscle spasms lock Gavin's chin. He wills relaxation into the seized muscles. Approaching the last water jump Gavin's right thigh knots. A buckling knee ahead forces the American, Kelly, to shift and hit Gavin's foot. When off balance, Gavin brushes the faltering Vasilov. A wizened official raises a red flag.

Gavin's sharp, short stride in catching balance realigns his nervous pathways, and he is back in control. Keeping a low crouch, he cradles his foot on the beam and allows his centre of gravity to advance before stabbing the ball of his foot against the receding barrier. He shoots out to a shallow landing. His momentum carries him past a stalled Nelson. Only Korir is ahead. Approaching the last hurdling obstacle, Korir shuffles his steps. But Gavin without breaking stride skims over to gain a metre on Korrir. I've got it! He assures himself as pain from his muscles pierces his very soul. The vision of a gold medal dangling from his neck is clear. Although sensing he is alone, he dare not glance back. During the final 10 meters the crowd's crescendo provokes goose flesh over Gavin's entire body. But no shadows hound him on either side when he keeps his disintegrating nerves synchronized past the finish line.

"I've done it! I've done it! It was possible!" He utters as the medical attendants lead him away. His right thigh seizes. He walks to the recovery area like the happiest sciatic patient on earth. Here he closes his eyes and reflects on his career. One day at a time he did his thing through frigid winters and sun-drenched summers forging a controlled aggression that ruled supreme this day. Never has he been able to spark so effectively such shattered muscles. A gleeful feeling, eight years in the making, flushes through him.

A subdued conversation at his side commands his attention. An impeccably dressed official in an emerald green blazer mumbles sternly to Gavin's attendant. Gavin sees his guide's smile dissolve. She stands with a blank look, bows to the emerald jacket and then to Gavin before crossing the room to fetch Vasilov. She now escorts the third place finisher and joins the other attendants. They head for a room identified with a microphone, a pen, and a video camera above its entrance.

Gavin asks the nearest official, "What's happening?"

"Disqualification!"

"What?"

"Last water jump, problem. Referee disqualifies."

Gavin slumps in his chair; he tries to concentrate. His mind swirls. Yes—he remembers a red flag going up approaching the final water jump. He recalls contact with the bushy-haired Russian but he also knew he had no choice. He sits with his head in his hands, thinking. Everything clicked and yet it's gone. It can't be! He stands and starts searching for the athletes' exit. Along the hallway through a glass window he sees the media people hovering like buzzards around the three athletes he has beaten. A chill of despair numbs his body.

A figure approaches on the run, grabs, and hugs him. It's Tanner.

"Let's get another look at the replay!" Tanner says.

They rush back inside the stadium, ignore credential checkers, and gain access to the edge of the track. The replay shows Gavin's contact with Vasilov. Gavin is dizzy. He collapses against the corridor wall. He sinks to the floor, his head between his knees. He stares into space. Tears gather in the corners of his eyes.

Moments later the steeplechase results flash, "DISQUALIFICATION: GOSLING CAN." Tanner crinkles his face. When he turns, he can't find Gavin. Then he sees him slumped like a trashed dishrag on the cement floor.

"Gavin, Gavin," Tanner stoops and embraces him once more. "You ran a perfect race; you waited and it paid off. Whether we win the protest or not you still annihilated them, and all experienced observers know it. "

Gavin forces a smile, "Protest, what do you mean?"

"We saw the American nick your foot forcing you off stride before you hit Vasilov. You couldn't see it on the big screen but they have cameras from all angles; the jury will spot it. Sandstrom is filing a protest."

Thoburn, on learning of Gavin's disqualification, uses his accreditation to get to the Canadian team manager in the athletes' section. Thoburn, after introducing himself, says, "Hey, Sandstrom, you may wish to include this in your protest. It was taken at the water jump and has the American striking Gavin before he hit the Russian."

Sandstrom, who was frantically writing, stops, takes a glance up and says, "Just give me a minute will you—please. I've got less than thirty minutes to get this in." Sandstrom withdraws his pencil from the paper and asks, "What did you say? You have a video. No, no, they've their own tapes; they won't look at anything else." Sandstrom returns to scratching a few more notes as the proper phrasing hits him.

"This tape shows exactly what happened. I could only look at the tiny playback, but even there you see Kelly move into Gavin. I'll leave it with you," Thoburn says and places the tape beside Sandstrom who is not paying attention.

"Look," Sandstrom says, "keep it will you."

Thoburn curses silently, shakes his head a couple of times, and walks away. Sandstrom takes fourteen minutes to write the protest. He checks his watch, still nine minutes before the deadline for filing. Being a meticulous man he reviews the rulebook under protests once more to insure everything is technically right. What's this? He asks himself when he reads, "The jury shall consult all other available evidence." His eyes dart up but Thoburn has vanished. Geez, I'm stupid, he says to himself, and whacks the base of his palm against his forehead. He rereads his appeal and signs it. When he picks up his kit bag beside his seat, he notices Thoburn's tape. He scoops it and sprints as fast as his fifty-four-year-old legs will carry him to the competition secretariat.

He meets Richard Pearce whom he has known for thirty years and hands him the protest form, the protest fee of fifty American dollars, and Thoburn's tape. "Look Richard!" Sandstrom says, and shows him his opened I.A.A.F. rulebook at the relevant passage. "A guy named Thoburn, a photographer working on Toronto's bid for the '96 Games, took some video shots precisely in front of the water barrier which, he says, shows Kelly caused it all. It may be obscured on the Games' cameras because the athletes on the water jump approach ran from the bright sun, into the darkness of the roof 's overhang."

"Thanks, thanks! I can't vote when a Canadian's involved, but I can contribute to the discussion."

Stadium viewers now notice a flashing of UNOFFICIAL beside the 3000-metre steeplechase standings. The Olympic Game's jury of appeal assemble in the referee's room to view the competition videos.

Mr. Gladbourough, from Great Britain, chairs the meeting. Richard has submitted Sandstrom's protest but keeps the tape as a last resort. Gladbourough scans the protest again, reads it to the group, and asks the technician to play the competition tapes taken of the water jump. Three reruns meet a stony silence.

"Well, gentlemen," Gladbourough says, "we've seen the evidence upon which the referee made his decision. I think it's rather straightforward. As usual those countries involved must abstain from voting. Barring further evidence, I'm calling the vote."

"One moment, please," Richard says, "I've a video taken from the photographers' trench which I'm told provides a different perspective and accounts for the sudden movement of the Canadian athlete; with your permission, I'll put it on."

Richard immediately walks to the playback machine and hands the tape to the technician who inserts it.

"Highly irregular" ... Gladbourough starts mumbling but the eyes of the jury scrutinize the monitor. Gasps, then sighs erupt when they see Kelly's stumble provoke Gavin's shift into Vasilov.

Richard pumps his fist a couple of times, and slips out of the jury room looking for Sandstrom, Gavin or Tanner hoping he will get word to one or all before the official release.

"Ladies and gentleman the original winner has been reinstated as victor in the 3,000-metre steeplechase. The official results are now posted on the electronic scoreboard."

Thirty minutes later Gavin fulfills the pledge he made after watching Baumann win at the Los Angeles Games; he floats to the highest height of the Olympic medal podium. One hundred thousand spectators stand for the playing of "O Canada". Gavin isn't sure if he sheds tears of relief or of joy but now it doesn't matter.

The End